AS GOOD
AS DEAD

AS GOOD AS DEAD

PATRICIA H. RUSHFORD

Revell

Grand Rapids, Michigan

Published by Fleming H. Revell
a division of Baker Publishing Group
P.O. Box 6287, Grand Rapids, MI 49516-6287

Printed in the United States of America

Library of Congress Cataloging-in-Publication Data
Rushford, Patricia H.
    As good as dead / Patricia H. Rushford.
        p.   cm. — (Angel Delaney mysteries)
    ISBN 0-8007-3075-5 (pbk.)
    1. Policewomen—Fiction. 2. Missing persons—Fiction. 3. Brothers and
sisters— Fiction. I. Title. II. Series.
PS3568.U7274A93 2005
813'.54—dc22   2005012673

ONE

C ade stepped over the dead witness, annoyed that the guy hadn't fallen where he'd shot him. Like a wounded bear, John Stanton had growled and staggered out of the bedroom. Cade had to hustle to steer clear of him. The last thing he needed was blood evidence on his designer suit.

Stanton had finally come to the end of himself beside the sofa. The blood trail made the job far too messy, and Cade hated messy murders. He wouldn't attempt to clean it up, of course. No need. Let the crime scene investigators have their fun. They'd find no evidence to link him to the crime.

Fortunately, the witness's so-called bodyguard had gone down immediately. He lay in an ever-darkening blotch on the champagne carpet in the bedroom. Nice and tidy. The guard's name was Ted Wheeler, a young guy, just out of college—a wannabe cop with an attitude. Cade felt a twinge of guilt over that one. The kid never saw it coming.

Cade brushed his irritation and guilt away and set his sights on more important matters. The hotel room bar offered a number of possibilities. He selected a small bottle of Jack Daniels, poured a shot into a clean glass, and then settled onto the bar stool. His watch told him he had a five-minute wait—providing the assistant DA showed up according to schedule. This one he wasn't looking forward to, but he had contracted for all three men, which seemed like overkill to him. *Overkill.* He smirked at the pun.

"Since when do you need a drink for courage?" Cade leveled his gaze at his reflection, taken aback by the broad nose and high cheekbones he'd fashioned out of the flexible plastic substance that served as a mask. When he met the concern in his dark brown eyes, he looked away, staring instead into the amber liquid before bringing it to his lips. Disgusted, he tossed back the contents, closing his eyes as the whiskey burned his esophagus on the way down.

He'd had no serious qualms about offing the two stiffs keeping him company, especially Stanton. The guy was a sleazeball. His concern lay in killing Luke Delaney.

Cade wasn't a religious man; no one would ever accuse him of that. He preferred to call the feeling in his gut intuition, or maybe just plain logic. He supposed he might even call it a conscience, though after all these years as a hired gun, he doubted he had one. Still, even a hit man had his limits.

Several things bothered him about the job. Delaney was a decent sort. He had a law degree from Harvard and had graduated at the top of his class, and he now worked as the assistant district attorney in Lee County. Delaney's father and best friend were cops, and his little sister, Angel, still in college, was heading in the same direction. Shooting Delaney would probably mean a relentless search for his killer by all three of them. Though Cade prided himself in leaving no evidence, he worried that his precautionary measures wouldn't be enough. He had already made certain that all traces of the request to kill Stanton and Wheeler had been eliminated. Still, no system was foolproof. He stared at the glass in his hand and took it over to the sink to wash away all traces of DNA, still ruminating over his would-be third victim.

To make matters worse, one of Luke's three brothers was a minister at St. Matthews Church in Sunset Cove, Oregon. Cade had a thing about taking out religious men and their families. No doubt, his reluctance reached back into his childhood—his father, a priest, had taught him a healthy respect for the church and everything connected with it. And Delaney was connected to the church in a big way. Even now, away from his family and living in Fort Myers, Florida, he went to church every Sunday.

Cade couldn't forget that two of Delaney's brothers had money—enough to keep an investigation going for years. And the family was Irish-Italian, like his mother. Cade shook his head. He rarely let sentimentality enter into his work, but this was more than sentimentality. He was getting some definite warnings urging him to take heed.

"On the other hand," Cade told his image, "Delaney's death would put another hundred grand in my pocket. Not exactly pocket change."

At exactly 7:30 a.m. a key card clicked into the slot on the door. Cade stiffened and drew his weapon, a Beretta he'd toss into the swamp along Alligator Alley, where it would never be recovered. The handle turned down, and the door swung open. Cade stepped out of sight and waited. Delaney would have to walk all the way into the room in order to see the dead witness. Sweat beaded his upper lip as he waited. He hated the indecision. With sudden insight, a smile curled his lips. He had the perfect solution.

Luke hesitated outside the door before inserting the key card his boss had given him. A premonition and an urge to run came over him. He wouldn't follow those urges, however; couldn't afford to. He'd come here to escort Stanton to the courthouse, where he would testify against the Penghetti brothers, who allegedly ran one of the biggest syndicated crime rings in the country. Drugs, theft, fraud, extortion, murder, you name it.

Alton Delong, his boss and the DA, had been working for years to put the Penghetti brothers behind bars. Now the DA's office had them, and no amount of money could buy their freedom—at least Luke hoped so. He thought it unfortunate that the bulk of their success in this case lay with one witness. And he didn't especially like the idea that he'd been asked to fetch the guy.

Luke inserted the key card, and when the light blinked green, he pressed down on the handle and pushed open the door.

"Stanton? Ted?" A stifling heaviness moved into Luke's chest as he stepped inside the hotel room and let the door close behind him. Standing in the hallway, he glanced at the closet to his left and the bathroom to his right. Beyond him was the suite with its private bedroom and another bath. Luke tried to convince himself that he had nothing to worry about—that his imagination was working overtime. But he couldn't deny the overwhelming feeling that something had gone terribly wrong. The suite was far too quiet.

Maybe they'd gotten their wires crossed and the witness and bodyguard were already gone. Or maybe they were in the bedroom and hadn't heard him. Luke moved forward. "You guys ready to go?"

His question was met with dead silence. Luke felt rather than heard a presence off to his left. The heaviness in his chest intensified as his gaze captured the man holding a gun and then flitted to the floor where John Stanton lay. Luke swallowed back his terror and saw his future die as his gaze followed the trail of blood into the bedroom. From where he stood he could see the guard and his blood-soaked uniform. Everything inside Luke told him to run, but logic told him it was too late. The killer would have a bullet in his chest before he could turn around. Better to at least try to get some answers and hope he'd have better odds of surviving if he postponed the inevitable.

"Who are you?" Luke managed to ask.

"Your savior," the man answered. "And I don't think your guys here are going anywhere—leastwise not to court."

"How did you get in here?" Luke sucked in a long, steadying breath and raised his hands. The killer didn't answer but kept a steady gaze on him, gun trained, ready to shoot. Only he didn't fire. *Why not just get it over with?* Within seconds the gun would explode, the bullet would penetrate vital organs, and Luke would take his last breath. And with no witness, the Penghetti brothers would go free.

Luke memorized the man's features and the raspy quality of his voice. Broad nose, tan skin, blond hair—dark at the roots—coffee-colored eyes, about six-four, around 230 pounds, muscular. The suit was expensive, perfectly cut. He wore latex gloves and had covered his shoes with the kind of booties crime scene investigators wore to keep the crime scene from becoming contaminated.

Luke felt certain he'd never seen the guy before, yet there was something oddly familiar about him.

Not that identifying him would serve any purpose. The guy was obviously a professional, which meant he was wearing a disguise. *And you won't live to tell anyone about him.* Luke settled his gaze on the floor and prepared himself for the inevitable.

"I don't usually talk to my victims before I shoot them," the killer said. "For you I'm making an exception."

Luke's head rose as he glared at the man. "I don't get it."

The killer sighed and seemed almost friendly. "I don't get it either, Luke. All I can tell you is that my client wants you dead, but my gut says I shouldn't kill you."

"Your client," Luke spat out the words. "Which one of the Penghetti brothers would that be? Bobby or Rick? Or maybe they're both in on it."

"It doesn't matter." His lips spread in a calculating smile. "This is how it's going down. As I said, I'm your savior. You are walking out of here, my friend. You won't contact anyone. You will disappear without a trace, and I'll tell my boss I threw your corpse in the swamp along with the gun I used to kill you."

"Why . . . ?"

"You'll leave your fancy little Corvette, your apartment, and everything you own." He waved the gun. "Turn around and put your hands behind your back."

Confused, Luke did as he was told. The killer snapped a pair of metal cuffs around his wrists, then patted him down for a weapon. The action seemed automatic, as though he'd been trained in law enforcement.

"I don't carry a weapon."

"Just making sure." He captured Luke's wallet and put it in his jacket pocket, then took his cell phone and keys, along with the key card Luke had used when he entered the room. He tossed the key on the bar.

Luke gritted his teeth, wanting to argue with him but worried the man might change his mind. *I have no intention of disappearing.*

The sneer returned. "Don't be stupid, kid," the hit man said as if he knew Luke's thoughts. "I'll get away with it, and you will disappear—unless you want to go to prison for the murder of your two friends here."

"There's no way anyone would believe I killed them."

"I wouldn't be too sure. Everyone can be bought, and you're no exception. Besides, there will be no evidence of my having been here." The killer pressed a glass into Luke's hand, then set it back on the bar. "Whereas, the evidence is rather clear that you were here."

"You're crazy." This time his thoughts did escape his lips, and Luke wished he could take them back.

The man ignored his comment. "Certain people want you dead, and your only option, if you want to stay alive, is to disappear. I'm giving it to you straight, kid; you'll need a new identity. I'm giving you one chance and only one to escape. You surface anywhere, and you're a dead man."

"I still don't—"

"You don't have to get it. Just take my word for it. Like I said, Luke Delaney is a dead man. He no longer exists, got that?" Without waiting for an answer, he continued. "The cops will find these guys within the hour, but you'll be long gone. CSI will have evidence that you were here. There'll be questions as to your part in all of this. It won't take much to convince the powers that be that you sold out, killed Stanton and Wheeler, and ran."

"No one would believe that." Luke repeated the words again, but this time they hung limp in the air.

"Won't they? Better men than you have caved to a big payoff. Besides, I need a fall guy. A call to the press implicating Luke Delaney should do it."

Luke shook his head. The killer was already talking as though he didn't exist. "This is insane. Why don't you just kill me?"

"Because it suits my purposes not to. As an added incentive for your cooperation, know this: if Luke Delaney surfaces in any way, shape, or form—if there's any attempt on Delaney's part to talk to the cops or anyone else—I start picking off his family. Maybe I'll start with the youngest." His lips curled in a sinister smile. "Angel, right? Of course, she's too pretty to just kill . . ."

Luke strained to pull free of the tight cuffs. "You touch her and—"

"Your disappearance is her life insurance."

"Why are you doing this?"

The hit man shrugged. "I don't think it's wise to kill you just now. On the other hand, I can't let Luke Delaney slip out of my hands. I have a reputation to preserve and money to collect."

"What's the going rate these days for exterminating people?" Luke gritted his teeth.

"Not nearly enough." The man took a step back and leveled the gun. "Now it's up to you. You can live as long as you're someone other than Delaney. Or I can kill you right here and now. Your choice."

"I'll go." Luke would take life, but he vowed to get this guy and put him away if it took a lifetime. There had to be a way to turn the tables on the Penghetti brothers and their hit man.

"Smart move. But remember, if I hear that Luke Delaney has surfaced, I go after his kid sister. Is that clear?"

"Perfectly." Luke saw no choice but to go along with the man's wishes—for now. There had to be a way out. Maybe as they left, he could signal one of the hotel security guards.

"Good. You and I are going to walk out of here together. And don't get any ideas about alerting anyone." The gunman lifted his jacket, showing Luke a badge identifying him as a law officer for Lee County. He took Luke's arm and propelled him forward, the gun barrel tucked in against Luke's ribs.

In the hallway, the man slipped off the gloves and the booties and tucked them into a small pack he wore around his waist. Luke noticed a heavy gold ring on his right ring finger with a garnet center and two small crosses that were carved on each side of the stone. A class ring, maybe? Luke stored it in his memory along with other details he'd give police when he had the opportunity.

They took the stairs down to the third floor, where the killer pulled open the heavy metal door. In the open doorway, he unlocked the handcuffs and shoved Luke into the hotel's parking garage. Luke fell forward, landing on his hands and knees. The door slammed shut, and when Luke looked back, the man was gone.

paused briefly to look at the red 1972 Corvette parked in the driveway. Luke's car.

Luke had graduated from Harvard Law School with honors and moved to the Fort Myers area, where he took a job as assistant DA in the district attorney's office. Everyone was so proud. But then came the terse note telling the family he was leaving and not coming back, and they were not to worry or try to find him. The note read like a will. In it he'd asked Angel to take care of his car.

All she knew about his disappearance was that Luke had been involved in some sort of high-profile case before he disappeared. Authorities seemed convinced that he'd killed a key witness and a guard, then fled. Their family never believed that story, and she doubted the people who worked with him did either. *What happened to you, Luke? I know you would never kill anyone, but why did you run?*

With her house torn up and Rachael not in need of her investigative skills at the moment, maybe she could do some digging. But where on earth would she start? The obvious place was Fort Myers, Florida, where Luke was last seen. Maybe she could go there and . . .

What am I thinking? She couldn't leave in the middle of moving to find a brother who apparently didn't want to be found . . . and who may no longer be alive.

No, that couldn't be true. She'd never allowed herself to think he might be dead and couldn't now. Luke was alive; she knew it in her heart. And there had to be a way to find him.

Angel left her longings behind and headed into the kitchen. Anna was singing and single-handedly unpacking Angel's things, treating each item as if it were a museum piece as she placed them in the appropriate drawers and cupboards.

"Ma, you shouldn't be working so hard." Angel opened the refrigerator and pulled out a pitcher of iced tea.

"Nonsense. Since when is getting my baby settled work?"

"Okay, Ma. Rule number one. If I'm going to live here, you have to stop calling me your baby."

Anna tossed Angel a knowing smile. "You'll always be my baby. Even when I'm an old woman and you're my age."

27

Angel shook her head. *Who am I kidding? Ma makes the rules—always has and always will.* "All right, just don't say it out loud." She lifted the pitcher. "Want some?"

"I would. Get some for Callen too, and let's go out on the deck. We could all use a break."

If taking a break herself would get her mother off her feet, so be it. Sometimes a person just had to make sacrifices. So Angel did as she was told and brought a drink in for Callen. "Want to join us on the deck?"

Callen thanked her for the tea. "As much as I'd love your company, I'd better keep working."

"Suit yourself."

The phone rang just as Angel was sitting down on one of the chaise lounge chairs on the sunny deck. "I'll get it." She set down her tea on the table and hurried back inside.

When she got to the phone, she picked up the receiver and said hello.

"Angel. Thank God you're home."

The caller was crying, and it took Angel a moment to recognize the voice. "Rosie? Is that you? For heaven's sake, take a breath and tell me what's wrong."

"It's Nick. He's been shot."

FIVE

A ngel spent the next thirty seconds telling Callen and her mother about the phone call and the next five minutes driving to the hospital with Callen. With lightning speed, he'd covered his T-shirt with his navy state police jacket and exchanged the hammer and tool belt for a gun and shoulder holster—like Superman sans the phone booth.

Since Callen had driven his unmarked blue Crown Victoria and couldn't take passengers, they took the Corvette, which seated only two people. Her mother hurried them along, saying she'd have Tim pick her up. "I'll be there as soon as I can. Call me the minute you hear anything."

Once in the car, Callen called his supervisor in Portland, getting the okay to help the local PD as necessary. As shorthanded as the Sunset Cove police department was, Callen would likely be assigned to head the investigation. He then spoke to dispatch, asking to be briefed and telling them he was en route to the hospital.

Angel watched Callen's expression as he made the call. He was all business now, a frown etching his face, making him look sterner, older than his thirty-three years. He was a cop first, like her father had been. That thought unsettled her. Did she really want to marry a man like Frank Delaney? Did she want to marry a cop?

All thoughts of Callen and her father fled when he hung up and cast a concerned look in her direction as he set his phone on the seat beside him and took her hand. His left hand gripped the steering wheel, leaving no doubt as to his rising adrenaline.

"What happened?" Angel asked. Rosie hadn't known or couldn't express many of the details. Rosie worked with the Sunset PD as a civilian receptionist, desk clerk, and secretary to the chief. She and Angel had been friends for years. And Rosie had been dating Nick for the past couple of months.

Callen shook his head. "I'm not getting much more than what Rosie told you. Nick was out on a patrol east of town and apparently walked into an ambush. Took two bullets but managed to get himself to his vehicle and call in. He's lost a lot of blood, Angel. It doesn't look good."

Callen pulled into a police parking space, the closest spot to the door. Inside the hospital, Callen showed his badge and got immediate entry into the emergency room. Angel followed close on his heels.

Rosie was standing just outside the drawn curtains.

"How is he?" Angel wrapped her arms around her old friend.

"They're getting him ready for surgery." Tears had puffed up Rosie's beautiful brown eyes, running her mascara and leaving black smudges on her cheeks. "They aren't telling me anything because I'm not family."

Angel rolled her eyes. Confidentiality laws—necessary, she supposed, but sometimes a terrible nuisance. "Did you tell them he has no family?"

"Yes, but . . ."

"Stay here." Callen swept the curtains aside and stepped into the cubicle. Moments later he came back out. The curtains swished open, and a man in green scrubs and a green surgical cap began pushing the stretcher out.

Nick's normally dark complexion was a pasty yellow. An IV bag dripped fluid through the clear plastic tubing and into the vein above his left wrist.

Angel felt as though a fist had slammed into her chest. Seeing Nick like this kicked off the flashbacks. Her best friend murdered in a Miami day care. Bullets shattering the window at Bergman's

Pharmacy as she and her partner pulled up to investigate a burglary. Blood pumping out of the boy . . .

She pulled herself back from the barrage of horrific scenes and focused on Nick. *Please, God, not Nick too. Let him be all right.*

He opened his eyes and offered Rosie a wan smile, his eyes glazed and unfocused. When Nick saw Angel, he held up a hand and caught her arm. The stretcher stopped. "Ange." He gasped and seemed to want to tell her something.

Barely able to hear him, she leaned closer.

"Luke," he whispered. "In trouble . . . Have to warn him." He let go of her and closed his eyes.

Nick, wait! What do you mean? She wanted to go after him, but it was too late. The stretcher went through the double doors and down the hall to the surgical suite.

Unsettled, she focused back on Callen and Rosie, who were both eyeing her with suspicion.

"What did he say?" Callen asked.

"I'm not sure." She wasn't lying. She'd heard the words clearly enough, or thought she had, but she needed time to process them.

Grim faced, Callen repeated what he'd learned from the doctor. Nick had taken three bullets in the chest. One had bitten into his vest above the heart but hadn't penetrated. The remaining two had entered just above his vest. One had angled down and punctured his left lung and apparently nicked a vessel. The second had entered his upper left chest, barely missing the aorta. The surgeons were going in to check out the damage and hopefully stop the bleeding.

"All we can do now is wait," Callen told them. "I'm heading out to the scene—see if I can pick up any information there. They've put a CSI detail on it, so hopefully . . ." He hugged Rosie and told her he'd be praying. Turning to Angel, Callen wrapped an arm around her shoulders and walked with her to the elevator.

"I know you want to come with me, but Rosie needs you. I'll tell you what I can as soon as I can." He kissed her lightly on the lips. His eyes said it all. He'd gladly have taken the bullets for Nick. Angel would have as well. It was a camaraderie they all shared. "I love you," he said.

"Me too. Be careful." Angel stared at the elevator doors after they closed him in. He knew her well. She had wanted to go out to the crime scene. But he was right, Rosie needed her, and truth be told, she wanted to stay there for Nick.

Angel called her mother as promised to let her know about Nick's condition, then went back to the surgery waiting area, where Rosie was sitting arms crossed, eyes closed, leaning forward. The waiting room was full of cops now, some from every agency in the area. Anyone who wasn't at the crime scene or needed elsewhere was waiting, pulling for Nick. Many of them talked to Rosie and Angel, offering sympathy and positive comments and prayers. Bo Williams from the sheriff's department came in. "He'll pull through. Nick's as tough as they come." Bo brought them both a cup of coffee and, after getting some for himself, took a chair next to Rosie. "I called your mama, Rosie," he said.

"Thanks. Is she coming?"

Bo nodded, his dark skin a sharp contrast to the white Styrofoam cup. "Your mother, my mother. By nightfall I suspect the whole family will be here."

Angel thumbed through an outdated *People* magazine but set it down when her mother and Tim arrived. Her brother was wearing his clerical collar and, after talking to Rosie and the others, gathered a group to pray.

Angel couldn't help but wish there was something she could do besides pray. Nick had been ambushed, and whoever had shot him knew he'd be wearing a vest. Knew where the vulnerable areas were. The shooter just missed the aorta, hitting slightly above the heart. If the bullet had hit Nick just right, he would have bled out immediately. This had been a deliberate attempt to kill him. But why?

Once again, she wished she were an active duty cop and not an outsider. She wanted to be out running down clues and looking for the shooter. Did the shooting have something to do with Luke? It must have. Why else would Nick have mentioned Luke's name?

"I'm distributing Luke's picture," Callen said. "He's wanted for questioning, and hopefully we'll get some response."

"He'll be arrested?" Angel didn't much like that idea, but Callen was right. Alerting the police nationwide was perhaps the best way to get to Luke before the killer did. She took the photo facsimile back from Tim, folded it in half, and tucked it into her purse.

Their food came, and they ate—or tried to. As much as she loved the food at the Burger Shed, nothing tasted good. Callen and Tim had no problem devouring their meals, however. Callen had ordered tomato soup and a vegetarian sandwich with sprouts.

Angel eyed Callen's meal with disdain. "You do know you could be shamed out of law enforcement for eating a healthy lunch like that, don't you?"

He chuckled. "I've been teased a time or two, but I'll take my chances."

She raised her hands in mock surrender. Tim, she noticed, had ordered healthier as well.

She picked up a limp fry and dipped it in catsup but didn't eat it. Sighing, she pushed her plate forward and got up. "I'm going home."

"I don't think you should tell Ma about all this," Tim said, holding his half-eaten turkey and cheese on whole wheat bread only inches from his mouth.

"I wasn't going to. She has enough to worry about. Talking about Luke would just upset her."

Callen caught her arm as she went to pass him. "I'm knocking off early today so I can get some more work done on the house."

She nodded, pausing to massage his shoulders. "I'll pick something up at the store for supper."

"You don't need to. I'll cook." He tipped his head back.

"Good." Though she didn't much feel like having company, even Callen's, she smiled. "That'll be nice."

If Callen noticed her dour mood, he didn't comment. He and Tim were talking about the remodel before she was even out of earshot. Angel hiked back up the hill to the church and climbed into her Corvette. Make that Luke's Corvette.

Instead of going home, she went back to the hospital. Nick had claimed he didn't know where Luke lived, but maybe he knew where Luke had been staying while in Sunset Cove. The manager of the place had probably gotten Luke's license plate number and ID. There had to be some way to find him, though at the moment her prospects seemed hopeless.

NINE

The watcher spotted his image in the window and had to smile. He had the perfect disguise. So what if the hair hadn't turned out exactly as he'd planned. This was even better. He'd read once that one of the best ways to hide was to be obvious and flamboyant.

He looked beyond his image to the hospital bed where Nick Caldwell lay. He'd failed with his first attempt to kill the cop, but he wouldn't miss again. He'd had both men in his sights the day of the funeral, but he'd had to go buy that stupid camera, and when he'd gotten back to the motel both their cars were gone. He'd driven all over town trying to find them.

He rubbed his hands together. His boss was getting impatient. It had taken him a couple of days to find Caldwell and figure out what to do. His plan had been perfect. No way should that cop have lived. He could've sworn Caldwell had died out there on that deserted road. Fortunately, the papers had kept him informed. And he had taken his time to devise another plan. Caldwell wouldn't survive this time.

Once the cop was dead, he had to figure out how to find Luke Delaney. The guy was probably long gone. He'd have to track him down somehow. Maybe when Delaney found out his buddy had been shot, he'd come back.

The watcher dismissed Delaney for now and focused instead

on killing the cop. Sooner or later Caldwell's pals would leave. Night would come and the visits would stop, and then he'd make his move. He patted the hypodermic needle in the pocket of the white lab coat. A lethal dose of digitalis should do the trick. The medical examiner would blame his death on medication error. No one would link him to the "mistake."

TEN

Walking down the corridor, Angel stepped around a thin man in green scrubs and a lab coat who was pushing an empty wheelchair. His hair was an odd shade of orangey blond. Everyone was into coloring their hair these days, and some of the effects were just plain weird.

The guard outside Nick's room gave her a nod as she approached. He'd been there earlier this morning when she'd had to show her ID. He'd checked the list of acceptable visitors and let her in. Looked like Joe Brady wasn't taking any chances. Not that getting past security was all that difficult. One could pretend to be a doctor or nurse or an aide and easily gain entry.

The thought brought her up short. She stepped back into the hall. The guy with the wheelchair was gone; so much for her suspicious meanderings.

Nick was alone this time around. "Hey." He seemed more alert and in less pain.

"Hey, yourself. Where's Rosie?"

"I sent her home. Figured I could do without round-the-clock visitors." He used the handheld control unit to raise the head of his bed.

"Hmm. You must be feeling better."

"A little. Just figuring out how to move so it isn't quite so painful. And they put me on pain pills instead of the hard stuff."

Angel nodded. "You up to talking some more about Luke?"

"Ah, give me a break, Ange. Riley was just here asking all kinds of questions. Why don't you talk to him?"

"Did you tell Callen anything you didn't tell me?"

"How would I know? I've been too far out of it to remember much."

"Nick, this is important." She told him about the twins and their sudden trip to Florida. "Did you talk to them about Luke?"

"No." He ran a hand through his already disheveled hair. "They've talked about Luke from time to time. After your dad died, they were all saying how sad it was that your dad hadn't been able to see Luke before he died. Maybe that triggered something for them. All I know is that right after Luke disappeared they hired a PI to find him, but as far as I know they never located him. I never told them anything."

Angel gripped the railing. "After the funeral, when you talked to Luke. Did he say where he was staying?"

"I went to his motel room, but only for a few minutes while he got his stuff. We went to get something to eat, and he took off from the restaurant."

"Which motel?"

"What are you doing, Ange? You need to stay out of this."

"I can't. I'm a detective, remember? Please, Nick. I thought if I could find the place where he stayed, I might be able to get a license number. Most places want that when you check in."

He sighed. "Ask Callen."

"Did you notice the plates on Luke's car?"

"No, they were too dirty. He didn't want anyone to see them, and he doesn't want to be found. If I'd known there would be trouble, I would've arrested him. He asked me not to say anything about his being here, and like a dope I went along with him."

"Come on, Nick, tell me where he stayed. Maybe I can find something. I could stop at every motel between here and Newport, but that'll take forever, and we need to find him."

"All right. He was at the Sea Captain. It's almost to Lincoln City. I doubt it will help, though."

"Thanks. I owe you one." Angel planted a kiss on his cheek

and left. On her way out she made it a point to check out every person she passed, partly to keep her eyes open for anyone remotely resembling Luke. If Luke had come back to see Pop after the heart attack, he might come to see Nick now. She saw no one resembling her older brother. But that didn't mean he wasn't there.

Angel headed north toward Lincoln City and pulled into the parking lot at the Sea Captain. Armed with the photo of Luke, she went into the office. A short, stout man came out to greet her. "Looking for a room?"

"No, but I'm hoping you can give me some information on someone who stayed here. I'm a detective, and I'm looking for this guy." She unfolded the photo.

With wrinkled forehead, he studied the picture. "You're the third one to come around here asking about him. There was another guy asking about him a few days ago, then a little while ago a detective came by."

"What did he look like?"

"Skinny, dark hair. Said this guy had left something at his restaurant, and he wanted to return it. Wanted an address."

"Did you give it to him?"

"I don't have one. This guy you're looking for. Is he a criminal or something?"

"No, he's my brother."

"Humph. Can't tell you much. Signed in as Hal Perkins. He was here last Saturday. Seemed nice enough. Didn't give us any trouble."

"Did you verify his name with a driver's license or credit card?"

"Nope. Seemed like he was in a hurry. Paid cash up front, so I figured it didn't matter."

"Did he give you a license plate number?"

"Yeah, I gave it to the detective who came by." He read off the number, and Angel wrote it down. Oregon plates. She doubted Luke would be hiding out in Oregon. Probably a rental car.

"Thanks. Can you remember anything about him? Anything at all?"

He poked a finger in his ear and tipped his head to the side. "Nope."

An older woman wearing glasses and a muumuu-type dress came up to the desk and glanced at the photo. "What's going on?" She looked from Angel to the photo and back again.

"Do you recognize this man?" Angel asked.

"She says he's her brother," the man said.

"Sure. I talked to him once. He was going swimming and needed a towel. Nice man—seemed sad. Said he was here for a funeral."

Angel's heart leaped to her throat. "Did he say anything else, like where he was from?"

Her face wrinkled. "I don't recall. Told me he missed his wife and his little girl." She glanced at the picture again. "I can't remember for sure, but I'm thinking he might have mentioned Idaho."

His little girl? Idaho? Angel thanked them and gave them one of the new cards Rachael had ordered for her, the ones that said she was a private investigator. "If you think of anything else he might have said, even in passing, please call me."

The woman nodded, took the card. "Like I said, I only saw him that once and for just a few minutes."

Angel left, her mind racing with possibilities as she pointed the Corvette toward home. She couldn't count the number of times she'd tried to figure out where Luke might have gone. Early on, she'd written down a number of possibilities. One of them had been Sun Valley, Idaho. Luke loved the mountains and water, and sports, especially swimming and skiing. He'd talked about getting a condo in Sun Valley and working there, but when the job came up in Fort Myers, he'd taken it, saying he planned to spend all of his spare time at the beach.

Angel had wanted to visit him in Fort Myers during spring break in her last year of college. He disappeared before she had a chance. Nick was right; gaining this information might prove useless. If Luke didn't want to be found, he certainly wouldn't be using his real name or license plate number. Was there any way to find him? He had to have left a clue of some sort.

Did he really have a child? Or had that been a ruse too? Angel had never even considered the possibility that Luke might have married. And a little girl. What if that part was real? Maybe he'd talked to the woman at the motel in a vulnerable moment. Angel clung to the possibility.

Callen's SUV was already parked in the driveway when she arrived. Sporadic pounding came from the back of the house. The mail truck had driven away just as she arrived, so Angel pulled into the driveway and walked back to the road to check the box. Bank statement, a *Coastal Living* magazine, a postcard inviting them to list the house with Milestone Realtors. Intent on a card with a California postmark, she almost didn't see the Priority Mail envelope leaning against the wall next to the screen door.

She picked it up, wondering who'd sent it. No return address, just square black printing that read "Luke Delaney" and a postmark from Portland. Her heart hammered and her stomach clenched—and her police training took over. Heavily taped, no return address. And according to Nick, Luke was in danger. She carefully set the envelope on the wicker table and went inside. Tossing the rest of the mail on the small end table, she closed the door softly behind her. Her gaze took in the empty room, the silent kitchen. Smells emanating from it promised a scrumptious dinner. "Ma?"

Getting no response, she padded back to the master bedroom, where Callen was working.

"She's out in the garden." Callen glanced up at her, and his smile faded. "What's wrong?"

"Good. I mean, I'm glad she's out there." Angel peered out the window and, satisfied that her mother wouldn't overhear, told Callen about the package. "Maybe I'm paranoid with what's been going on, but . . . I have a weird feeling about it."

"Then we'd better have it checked out." Callen walked with her back to the front door and peered out the window.

"We don't want to walk out there," he said. "We'll want the CSI team to go over the porch, and the less contamination, the better."

That was one of the things she loved about Callen. He took

her concerns as seriously as he would a colleague's. Pulling his cell phone out of his pocket, he called the Oregon State Lab and asked that an explosives team be sent out. When he'd hung up he glanced at the kitchen. "They'll be here in about an hour. In the meantime we'll have to decide what to do about Anna."

"Decide what to do about me?" Anna wandered into the living room. "What have I missed?"

Breath rushed out of Angel's lungs. *Great. Just great.* The last thing her mother needed was to see that letter or the bomb squad.

"You're not thinking about sending me to some retirement home, are you?"

"Of course not, Ma. Callen was just . . ."

"We were wondering what you might want to do while we're on our honeymoon," Callen told her.

"You're getting married? Oh!" She clasped her hands, which wasn't easy with a cast covering much of her right hand. "This is wonderful. You don't have to worry about me."

Angel glared at Callen. "Honey, you shouldn't get her hopes up like that. Ma, we were just talking. We're not getting married for a long time. By the time we do, you'll be back to your old self."

Callen winked at Anna. "Can't blame a guy for trying. Maybe you can talk her into making it sooner."

Anna chuckled. "I'll do my best."

"How about taking a ride with me?" Angel asked, trying to come up with a diversion. "Maybe we can pick up your granddaughters and get a cup of coffee and a treat at Joanie's. Callen is hammering up a storm, and I'd just as soon not be around to hear it."

Anna sighed. "That sounds nice. I haven't been out in a while, have I? And I'd love to see the girls. I'll get my jacket."

When Anna had gone to her bedroom, Angel wrapped her arms around Callen's waist. "Thanks. I didn't want to lie to her."

Callen kissed her nose. "You did good. Hopefully the team won't have to spend much time here. I'd rather you didn't come out this way. Any chance you could walk along the beach?"

"Sure. She should be able to make it there, but I may have to call you to come get us."

she lifted her gaze and squeezed Angel's hand. "We'd better see what Callen has planned for dinner."

Within minutes they had the oven on and heated. Callen, true to his word, had seen to everything. He'd made a luscious-looking lasagna, and all Angel had to do was put it into the oven. She'd bake the prepackaged sourdough bread and make a salad. Simple enough.

Dinner went amazingly well, considering that Angel still didn't know if the professor was for real or not. He was charming and entertained them with stories about law students, several of which featured Luke. If the man was an imposter, he'd certainly done his homework.

With suspicions still foremost on her mind, Angel spent most of the time wondering what could have been keeping Tim. She'd tried his home several times, but still no answer. Finally at 8:15, the phone rang. She jumped up from the table to pick it up.

"Angel, it's Tim."

"Where are you? I've been trying to reach you for hours."

"We were at the doctor's office first, then the hospital. Abby has the flu and a high fever. She can't keep anything down, and the doctor finally decided to hydrate her."

"Oh no. Is she okay?"

"She's weak and still running a slight fever. They're giving her an IV." He sighed heavily. "I just sent Susan and Heidi home. Heidi isn't feeling too well either. Hope she doesn't get what Abby has."

"I hope not. Tell Abby that Nana and I send our love." Visions of the little girl in the hospital room reminded Angel of Nick. "Have you seen Nick?"

"No, I haven't had time."

"Then you haven't heard the latest. Someone tried to kill him again. Callen is there."

"I can't believe it. No wonder there are so many cops around."

"I don't imagine you were able to do any research on you-know-who?"

"No, sorry. The professor was the last thing on my mind. When I got back to the office, Susan had called and I left right away."

"It's okay. I'm just glad Abby is all right. Look, don't worry about it. I think you may be right. I'll check it out myself later tonight or tomorrow. Just take care of my little niece."

"I plan to."

Angel hung up and gave her mother the rundown.

"You're sure she's all right?" Anna asked. "She doesn't have meningitis or anything? I've heard about little ones dying from that."

"Tim says it's the flu and she's dehydrated. I'm sure they're checking for everything."

"I hope so." She took her cup to the sink. "I'd like to go see her."

Dr. Hathaway looked concerned. "Is there anything I can do?"

Angel saw nothing but sincerity in his eyes, and she wondered how she could have made him out to be anything but what he was: Luke's favorite professor. "Thank you for offering."

"Prayer would be good," Ma said.

"Certainly." He stood. "Well, I should be going. I'll be moving on tomorrow, but I can't tell you how much I appreciate your hospitality. The meal was superb. I'm sorry I couldn't have met your Detective Riley, Angel. He sounds like a fine man."

"He is," Angel assured him.

"I'm glad you looked us up," Anna said as she walked him to the door. "It was wonderful to meet you and hear about Luke. It's been a long time since we've really talked about him."

The professor reached for Anna's hand and shook it. "And you, my dear Anna, must look me up if and when you come to California. I'd love for you to meet my family."

"I will."

"And that goes for you too, Angel."

"Thanks, Dr. Hathaway, but I don't think I'll be going to California any time soon."

After a few more pleasantries, the professor left. Angel finished cleaning up the kitchen, and then she and her mother drove to the hospital. As much as she wanted to, Angel didn't even try to see Nick. Instead they went straight to the pediatric ward to see Abby.

"Nana! Auntie Angel!" Abby seemed alert and rosy cheeked as she held out her arms for a hug.

Tim gave up his chair and offered it to Anna. "You two didn't have to come down here."

"Of course we did." Anna extricated herself from Abby's thin arms and handed her the small package she'd picked up at the drugstore on the way. Abby pulled the small, cuddly teddy bear from its wrapper and hugged it. "Oh, Nana, this is the bestest present I ever got."

Angel chuckled at Abby's delight, happy to see their worries were for nothing. Or maybe their prayers had been answered.

While the three adults chatted, Abby's eyelids grew droopy and she nodded off, Mr. Bear tucked under her arm. Anna looked almost as tired, as did Tim.

"We'd better go," Angel finally whispered. Her mother didn't argue.

"I'm glad we came," Anna said as they stepped onto the empty elevator. "Now at least I'll be able to sleep tonight."

"Amazing what a little hydration will do—and a teddy bear."

Once home, Angel fixed two cups of chamomile tea and brought them into the living room, where her mother sat in the recliner with her legs propped up.

"Have you heard from Faith, the reporter who was going to write that article on Pop?" Angel asked.

"No, which is odd. She told me the article would be in the paper within a couple of days and she wanted me to read it first."

"Hmm. Maybe she got sidetracked. I'll call her tomorrow, or maybe stop by her place." Angel yawned. She found herself hoping that Michael Penghetti had been the gardener and that Faith had gotten a picture of him.

"That would be nice, dear." After a long silence, Anna rose. "I'd like to sit out here with you, sweetie, but I'm exhausted."

"Then go to bed." Angel smiled. "You don't have to wait up with me. Callen should be here before long."

"I know. Good night, then."

"Good night, Ma."

Angel watched the fire flickering in the fireplace, missing Callen and wondering whether or not she should go back to the hospital.

Callen dragged himself in at around 11:00, saying he just wanted to say good night before heading home.

"No update? You're not going to tell me what happened?"

"Can it wait until morning?" Callen yawned and rubbed the back of his neck. "You'll be able to read about it in the papers or watch it on the news."

"Sure, but I'd rather hear about it from you. Maybe you could come by in the morning for breakfast?" As much as Angel wanted to hear about Nick and wanted to tell Callen what she and Rachael had talked about, she didn't have the heart to keep him up a minute longer. His five o'clock shadow was already turning into a full-fledged beard, and he could hardly keep his eyes open.

He nodded. "Thanks for not pressing." He kissed her lightly on the lips. "Dinner go okay?"

"Fine. The lasagna was fantastic."

"Sorry I couldn't meet the professor. Maybe tomorrow."

Angel shrugged. "Too late. Dr. Hathaway is leaving town in the morning."

"Sorry I missed him, then."

"We did have some excitement though." She told him about Abby and their visit to the hospital.

"Poor kid," he said. "I'll stop by to see her tomorrow when I go in to talk to Nick. See you in the morning. I'll come early and cook breakfast."

"You don't have to do that, Callen. My arm isn't that bad."

"No, but like I said earlier, I enjoy spoiling you and being indispensable."

The final good-night kiss brought too many longings to the surface. Not wanting to say good-bye, she stood on the front porch, watching him get into his car and back out. She sighed. Times like this she felt like giving in and agreeing to marry Callen. A summer marriage might not be a bad idea, after all. She loved him, so what was stopping her?

Too much unfinished business.

When his taillights disappeared around the corner, Angel stepped into the house and locked the door, then went back to the deck to bring in the things she'd left there earlier. Picking up a blanket and her glass, she felt a chill ripple up her spine and raise the hairs on the back of her neck. She scanned the area visible within the parameters of light, which barely reached the surf. The shadows seemed to take shape and sway.

Must be the wind. Or your imagination. Angel hurried back inside and slid the heavy door shut, locked it, and closed the vertical blinds.

SIXTEEN

The watcher stayed outside Angel's house for another half hour before finally trekking through the sand toward the car he'd parked half a mile away. He'd had to change his hair again and check out of his motel, all because the stupid cop had to go and wake up before he could inject all the digitalis.

Of all the bad luck. Twice now he'd had the opportunity to kill Caldwell, and twice something had happened to mess him up.

"Humph," he spoke into the wind. "It's almost as if the guy has a guardian angel or something. What are the odds of him surviving a shooting like that?" And today, he'd been this close. Only seconds more and the digitalis would have been in Caldwell's bloodstream.

His boss wasn't going to like this. Not one bit.

The watcher stuffed his hands into the pockets of his rain jacket. What was he going to do now? He'd messed up on Caldwell, and Luke Delaney was long gone. He should have stuck with dealing drugs and stealing. Murder wasn't his thing, and it showed. Everything would have been cool if his contact hadn't needed pictures. Well, he had a picture of Caldwell, and the guy looked real dead. Maybe he'd just send that picture in and be done with it. The watcher had the feeling his contact lived back East somewhere. He'd probably never know that Caldwell had survived. Could he chance it? The watcher brushed the sand off his shoes and slid in behind the wheel, then drove slowly through town, dialing his contact's number and waiting while it rang and rang. By the time someone answered, he was through town and heading toward Lincoln City. "Yeah, it's me."

His contact muttered something unintelligible. "You'd better have a good reason for waking me up in the middle of the night."

"Sorry, I forgot about the time change. What is it, three hours difference?"

More swearing and grumbling. "This better be important."

"It is. I got Caldwell, and I'm sending a picture tomorrow. Just tell me where to mail it."

The contact gave him a post office box in Orlando.

After hanging up, the watcher smiled. Within a day or two he'd have ten grand, then maybe he'd head to Mexico or something. Or maybe he'd work a little harder to find this Delaney guy. It would mean another ten grand, and he sure could use the money.

SEVENTEEN

Fewer things tasted better than Callen's macadamia nut pancakes with piña-colada syrup served with crisp slices of bacon. Even though the chef was a health nut and used nothing but the freshest ingredients, everything tasted great.

I could get used to this. Angel didn't say it aloud. *No sense encouraging him.*

Once he'd served Anna and Angel, Callen sat down and sipped at his coffee, then spread the syrup on his pancakes. Angel waited until he was half through eating before asking him about Nick.

He set down his fork and picked up his coffee cup. "According to the guard, Nick was asleep when a guy wearing a lab coat came in with a medication tray. He was wearing an ID tag that identified him as a doctor, so the guard figured he was okay. Things got chaotic after that. Nick woke up and saw the guy. Recognized his face right away and saw that he was injecting something into his IV. Nick yanked out the IV and started yelling for the guard. The so-called doctor yelled for a nurse and ran out of the room. The guard took one look at the blood pouring out of the IV site and passed out. Nick tried to stop the bleeding but wasn't doing a very good job of it. Some of the staff came running in and thought Nick was going nuts. He kept telling them to get the cops, and someone finally listened."

A laugh bubbled out of Angel. "Sorry. I know it isn't funny, but it sounds like something out of a Three Stooges movie."

"Funny to tell it, but not so funny when it was actually happening. I got a page from Joe saying one of his officers had responded to the call and asking me to meet him there." Callen shook his head. "The place was a disaster, bloody footprints all over the room. It'll take our CSI team weeks to figure out what went down. Nick says he's sure the same guy who shot him tried to poison him. We confiscated the IV tubing and are having the OSP lab check it. For a while we didn't know if Nick was hallucinating or dreaming or if it actually happened. He managed to pull out his chest tube in the process so he's not in the best shape. Still maintains that he saw the guy who shot him, only the hair was different, some weird shade of orange."

"Orange?" Angel nearly choked on her juice. "I wonder if that's the guy I saw at the hospital yesterday. He was pushing a wheelchair, and I didn't think much of it."

"You think it might be the same guy?"

"It's possible. How many guys have orange hair? Okay, these days quite a few. I thought he looked strange at the time, but maybe my intuition wasn't too far off. He had on green scrubs and a lab coat then and an ID badge."

"The guard said he'd seen him on the floor before."

Anna hadn't said a word and had barely touched her food. Callen apologized for all the morbid talk at the table.

"It isn't that. I just can't understand why anyone would go to such extremes to kill Nick." Anna drained her cup and announced that she was going to take a shower and go to the hospital to see Abby. "Thank you for a wonderful breakfast."

Angel watched her mother deposit her cup in the sink and shuffle out of the room, wondering how long it would take for the spark to come back to her eyes and to her smile.

"She'll be okay, Angel," Callen said.

"I know." Angel cut out a bite of pancake and put it into her mouth, savoring the luscious tropical flavors. "About Nick. I hope the security measures are tightened."

"They have been," Callen assured her. "It's hard, though. We'll keep the uniformed guard. Our guys are volunteering to do extra duty. We have a list of people who are allowed access to the room, and we've placed their names on the roster. Anyone else attempting to go in will be escorted to the police department. They have orders to act first and ask questions later."

"So, this guy got away?"

"I'm afraid so. By the time Nick was able to give an accounting, the guy was long gone. There are no doctors or nurses that fit his description. My suspicion is that our guy stole the identification and clothes out of someone's locker. He'd have to know who was on vacation, but that wouldn't be too hard to figure out. He was seen leaving the hospital, but we have no idea what he was driving or where he might have gone. We have an APB out on him and have given the news media a description."

Angel tried to picture the orange-haired guy and superimpose his features over the gardener's and the photos she had of the Penghetti clan. No luck. "I have something for you from Rachael." Angel told him about the information Rachael had gathered on the Penghetti family and went back to her room to get it. She wanted to keep the photos for comparison but would get copies from Rachael later.

He flipped through the folder. "Rachael did her homework. This is all duplicating what I already have, though."

"She thought it might. Do you mind if I keep these? I want to check the photos of the Penghetti brothers against the photos taken at the funeral."

"Sounds like a good plan," Callen said. "We've left several messages with the reporter, but she hasn't called back. And to be honest, we've been too tied up to follow through."

"I can track her down for you."

"Great. Just let me know what you find out."

After breakfast, Callen left for work and Angel did the dishes. She'd just finished when Anna joined her in the kitchen for a second cup of coffee. "How would you feel about my going to visit Gabby?" Ma asked.

"Did Dr. Hathaway put you up to this?" Angel tried to keep the annoyance out of her voice.

"Of course not. I told you yesterday about Gabby's letter."

"Oh, right. Do you want to go?"

"I think so. Lazing around here frustrates me no end. I see all these things that need to be done, and with my arm broken, I can't do most of them."

"I'm trying to help, Ma, but with all the remodeling . . ."

"You've been a tremendous help." She smiled. "Callen and I have even made a halfway decent cook out of you."

"Only halfway?" Angel chuckled, glad to have come that far. She'd never been much into domesticity, choosing to follow in her father's footsteps rather than her mother's. She was just beginning to learn the things she'd missed out on during her growing-up years. Like cooking and keeping house.

"Maybe a bit more. But you've a long ways to go before I'd say you were proficient in the kitchen."

"Well, at least I don't do takeout all the time like I used to."

"You didn't answer my question." Anna rested her cast on the table. "What do you think about my visiting Gabby?"

"I think you should go."

"Good. I found a great buy on a ticket online. I'm leaving on Sunday."

"Ma!" Angel laughed. "If you'd already made up your mind to go, why did you ask?"

Anna grinned. "I would have canceled if you didn't want me to."

"I want you to be happy." Angel put away the rest of the glasses. "You're not planning to see the professor while you're down there, are you?"

"I might. Do you have a problem with that?"

"Just that . . . Ma, he was hitting on you, and I don't trust him."

"Don't be silly, Angel. He was a perfect gentleman—and a married man." She paused. "Besides, I can't imagine you thinking . . ." Tears gathered in her dark eyes. "Honey, I'm certainly not interested in him, if that's what's concerning you. I loved your father so much. That's why I need to leave for a while. I can't bear being in this house right now. Every time I go into the bedroom, I'm

97

reminded of how sick he was and how he fell on me. I keep thinking there should have been something I could have done—some way to get to the phone."

Angel wiped her hands and circled her mother's shoulders with her good arm. "It doesn't do any good to blame yourself. There was no way you could have moved him. You know that. But I know what you mean. I blame myself too. If I had gotten here earlier, maybe I could have saved him."

Anna nodded. "You had no way of knowing. I doubt either of us could have made a difference." She sighed. "Guilt and self-blame are part of the grieving process, I suppose."

"Yes, but knowing that and believing it are two different things." Angel gave her shoulder a squeeze. "We have to keep reminding ourselves that it was Pop's time to go. And like Tim keeps telling us, he's in a better place."

Anna dug into her pocket for a tissue. "I know. I'm just . . . having a hard time. I want the crying to stop, and I want to get on with my life. I'm tired of buying tissues." She offered a wan smile, a pathetic laugh—just enough to break the somber mood.

"Me too." Angel needed a couple tissues of her own.

"Why don't we walk on the beach?" Anna sniffed. "And we can talk about my trip."

"It's raining."

"And your point is?"

Angel chuckled. She'd spent most of the days since her dad's death with her mother. Holding her when she cried. Walking when she needed to walk. Talking when she needed to talk. After the funeral, a friend had given her a book on helping someone through grief, and one of the most important things the author stressed was just going through it together and being there for one another.

Anna was still crying when they reached the packed sand. Angel knew it was going to be one of those days.

The rain washed away their tears and stung their faces, but on they walked. After a while, Anna turned back. "I think I have it out of my system now, or at least it's lessening."

"What?"

"The anger. He had no business dying on me when he did. I'd

"I'm not surprised by that. You were in high school back then and busy with your own friends. By the time we finished working at the camp, it was time to go back to school. I never heard about her after that, but they must have kept in touch."

She showed him the Coeur d'Alene list. "Any of these look familiar to you?" Angel asked.

He looked over the names. "Sorry. Like I said, he didn't give me much information. He didn't want to tell me anything, but his wife's name slipped out when we were talking."

"You've given me more than enough information. I'll find him."

"What then, Ange?"

"I don't know."

"Watch your back. If the killer knows Luke was here and if the same guy came after me, he could go after you too. And he could follow you to Idaho."

"I know what he looks like. And I can make sure I'm not followed."

"Yeah, the guy is ruthless. Look what happened to me—and that reporter."

"Have you heard anything about that investigation?" Angel sat back in the chair and carefully tucked the paper with the names on it into a pocket of her bag.

"Joe said the OSP is working all the angles. No word yet as to evidence or who they might be looking for."

"Callen said they had to look at Luke as a possible suspect." Angel bit her lip. "He wouldn't kill someone to protect his identity, would he?"

"Not the Luke I know—knew, but . . ." He shook his head. "No. Of course not. Luke's still the same great guy he was before he disappeared."

Angel nodded. "I hope you're right."

"When are you leaving?" Nick asked.

When? Now. Today. "I haven't thought it out completely. Should I fly over? Drive? I'll need my car," Angel said, thinking aloud.

"It'll take you seven or eight hours to get there."

"I could leave right away. Thanks, Nick. I'll keep you posted."

She got up from her chair. "One more thing: do you think I should tell Callen? I feel badly not keeping him in the loop."

"Tell him what you need to. Right now all we have is a few leads. You can worry about telling Callen if and when you find Luke. If you do find Luke, let him know what's going on and let him decide what to do." Nick held out a hand to her. Angel grasped it and bent over the railing to kiss his cheek.

"Be careful," he said.

Angel promised she would. She had to be. Luke's life depended on it.

Before leaving she took a few minutes to check out the Summerfield Gallery on the Internet. It took only moments to find Kinsey's website. She was listed as Kinsey Summerfield Sinclair. The artwork was impressive. She was located in the world famous Coeur d'Alene Resort and Conference Center. Checking out the white pages, she found Kinsey listed with Thomas Sinclair. Her heart beat far faster than it should have, and she could hardly breathe. Could Nick be right? Could the attractive woman featured as the owner be Luke's wife? Angel's sister-in-law?

After writing down the addresses and phone numbers, she closed down the computer and loaded up the car. *Am I doing the right thing, God?*

"I just hope I'm right and that Luke is safe," she said to herself as she locked the front door. Climbing into her Corvette, she remembered Callen's dog. Callen hadn't asked her to take care of Mutt, but maybe he'd taken for granted that she would. She drove the half mile to Callen's place and noticed a familiar white car parked out front. Angel rang the bell, and when the door opened, Mutt greeted her with his usual doggie enthusiasm. She scooped up the white wiggling bundle and cradled him in her arms. "Hey, fellow. Did you miss me?" He yipped, obviously telling her he had.

Callen's sister, Kath, laughed. "I missed you too."

"It's good to see you." Angel put the dog down and gave Kath a hug. "I didn't know you were coming."

"I'm surprised Callen didn't tell you. We agreed that I'd come down and house-sit while he was in Portland."

"No wonder he didn't ask me to take care of Mutt. I thought he assumed I would. I should've known he wouldn't forget something that important."

"You've got that right." Kath headed for the kitchen. "I'm glad you came by. Would you like some coffee?"

"Actually, I was just leaving town. I thought I'd better make sure Mutt was being taken care of."

"No worries. You're leaving town too? What is this, a mass exodus? Do you guys know something I don't?"

"Nothing like that. I have some business out of town." Angel wished she could confide in Kath. She liked Callen's sister and hated not being honest with her.

"Well, have a safe trip. Does Callen know you're going?"

"We'll be talking every day on the phone." She gave Kath and Mutt another hug as she left. Satisfied that Mutt and Callen's home would be well cared for, Angel headed north on 101 toward Lincoln City. On the way, she called Rachael to let her know where she was going.

"Call me twice a day so I'll know what's going on."

"Twice?"

"Think of it as insurance. If you miss a call, I'll call Callen. I don't like you going alone."

"All right, but I'll be fine," Angel said with much more conviction than she felt. Hanging up, she eyed the long line of cars behind her in the rearview mirror. She'd told Nick she'd be able to tell if she was being followed, but with so much traffic she'd have a hard time telling. On the other hand, traffic would thin out when she headed east from Portland. She'd just have to stay alert and watchful.

TWENTY-FOUR

C ade pulled off his earphones when Angel left Nick's room.
It had been a long morning but worth the wait. Truth be
told, he'd even appreciated Tim Delaney's sermon. Too bad
he'd never have that assurance of salvation Delaney talked about.
Cade was too far gone to entertain thoughts of saving grace.

In his youth, he'd occasionally fancied himself becoming a
pastor, like his father. Life had managed to destroy any chance
of that. God had allowed a madman to murder his father, and
for what? Cade never knew; no one did. The man had come into
their home one winter night, waving a gun, screaming obsceni-
ties. He'd fired five times, then turned the gun on himself, and
all the while Cade and his mother looked on, helpless, frozen
in place.

His brother had been the one to call the police. He'd been in
his room studying and heard the shots.

Over the years, Cade's grandfather had talked about forgiveness,
but how did one forgive such a brutal, unnecessary act? Anger and
bitterness had driven Cade far from the church. Perhaps he was
no better now than the man who had murdered his father. Some
would say he was far worse.

Salvation? Humph. Cade had killed far too many people for
that.

He brushed aside the memories and whatever remorse he might

have felt. His task would be finished soon. Thanks to Angel, he had all the information he needed for now. He'd drive back to Portland, return the rental car, and fly into Spokane. With any luck at all, he'd arrive in Coeur d'Alene and get to Luke Delaney before Angel did.

TWENTY-FIVE

t was dark by the time Angel got to Coeur d'Alene. Despite the headwind and rain coming up the gorge, she'd made good time, having only stopped three times for gas and food and to use the bathroom. Her last stop was at the city's first exit, where she stopped at a gas station to get directions. That had been ten minutes ago.

Now, she pulled into the lakeside resort where Summerfield Gallery was located. She'd start there and hopefully talk to Kinsey Summerfield Delaney. Or no, make that Sinclair. Kinsey was married to Thomas Sinclair. Angel had learned that much looking up the woman's gallery on the Internet.

Where had Luke gotten the name? Did Kinsey know who he really was? If she'd known him back in college, how could she not?

Exhaustion had long since settled in, clouding her brain and bringing her close to tears. Leaving her car with the valet, she grabbed her one rolling suitcase and her bag, then walked through the door that the bellman held open for her.

She tossed a thank-you over her shoulder and made a beeline for the front desk. On the way, she passed several shops, lingering for a moment at the Summerfield Gallery. The knots in her stomach seemed to tumble all over themselves at the thought of seeing her brother again. If Nick was right and Luke had come here, then this was her sister-in-law's art gallery. What was she like? Did Luke work here with her? When Angel came down for breakfast tomorrow, would she see him?

Don't get your hopes up. This may not be him at all. You'll find out tomorrow. Right now you need to get some sleep. Or at least some rest. Between the renewed adrenaline and the excitement of possibly finding Luke, she doubted she'd sleep all night.

The price of her room ended up being way beyond her budget. None of the smaller, less expensive rooms were available, but to her surprise, the desk clerk put her into an upgrade on the room for the same price. A nice gesture.

By the time Angel found her room, got into her pajamas, and brushed her teeth, she was more than ready for bed. Closing the curtains, she realized that her room overlooked the lake. Lights flickered in the harbor and across the dark water. "More than an upgrade," she murmured. This was definitely in the two hundred dollar or more a night range. The room was spacious and had a couch and a chair as well as a table and a desk. Angel yawned and tossed back the covers. Her concerns about not sleeping faded into oblivion.

Angel awoke when someone knocked on her door.

"Housekeeping."

The door opened, and a maid of Hispanic descent gushed out an apology in broken English. "I'm sorry. I didn't know—I knocked."

"Hey, it's okay. Don't worry about it." Angel sat up in bed, trying to get her brain engaged. "What time is it, anyway?"

"It is 11:00." The young woman backed out of the room. "I come back later."

"Right. Later." Angel dragged herself out of bed and hung out the do-not-disturb sign. She smiled and waved at the maid, then closed the door and padded to the small kitchen area, where she found a coffeemaker and the coffee to go with it. Once she'd put the coffee on, she used the facilities and took a long, hot shower. Waking up more fully brought the excitement and anxiety back again. Still wearing only a towel, she poured her coffee and sipped on it while she dressed. Angel had packed casual and put on her navy Dockers and a short-sleeved, lightweight sweater, white with a navy trim. What did one wear to confront a long-lost brother's wife?

If she is Luke's wife. Angel reminded herself that the woman might not be Luke's wife at all. Even though Nick had made the connection and it made sense, Thomas Sinclair may not be her brother.

"Don't get your hopes up, Angel." She pulled a brush through her still-damp hair, then, making sure she had her key, picked up her bag and left. She'd get some food first, then think about what she'd say to this Kinsey person. Hopefully the woman would be available and willing to talk.

Angel had tucked away Thomas Sinclair's name and address and the computer-generated picture of what Luke looked like now. Several things she knew, and those things were adding up, paving the way toward Luke. Luke had been at the funeral and talked with Nick. He'd mentioned Idaho in his discussion with the woman at the hotel where he'd stayed. And Nick seemed to think Luke was in serious danger from the same guy who'd tried to kill him. The reporter taking the photos at the funeral was dead. Possibly killed by the same man who'd shot at Nick. Faith's house had been torn apart, and Angel suspected the killer had most likely been looking for a photo of himself. Nick felt certain the man who'd been gardening at the cemetery that day was the one who shot him. Angel had seen the man twice and had practically memorized his features. She felt certain she'd recognize him if she saw him again. *Unless he's done something drastic to alter his appearance.*

Angel went into the dining room on the main floor and was offered a seat at the window, where she could watch boats come in and out of the harbor. As she followed the waitress, she glanced around at the other customers. No one looked the least bit suspicious. And no one resembled the gardener.

All the way to Idaho, she'd checked the cars and people around her. She'd seen nothing to indicate she was being followed. Of course, that didn't mean she hadn't been. Angel was well aware of ways to tail people without being seen.

Making herself relax, she studied the menu and settled for

eggs and toast with orange juice and coffee. Though her stomach rebelled at the sight of the food, she forced herself to eat. She needed the energy. And she needed courage—too bad that didn't come in the form of food.

When she finished breakfast, she braced herself for her encounter with Kinsey Summerfield-Sinclair. Angel paid the bill and then, nervous as a first-time actress, walked across the marble floor and through the enormous lobby with its comfortable-looking seating areas. Again she scanned the occupants. No one looked out of place or familiar.

Her heart hammered in her ears as she approached the gallery. She took a long, settling breath and stepped inside. As she slowly walked through the place, she pretended to examine the artwork, almost wishing she didn't have an agenda. She caught sight of a watercolor by Steve Hanks, one of her favorite artists. The scene depicted children examining something in a pond. So exquisite was the work that for a moment she was drawn into their innocence.

"Can I help you?"

The female voice jolted Angel out of her reverie, and she turned around quickly. She tried to smile and assess the woman all at once. She was close to Angel's age and height, only heavier. She had warm brown eyes and rusty brown hair that went beautifully with her tan and the yellow top she wore.

"Steve Hanks is one of my favorite watercolor artists." The woman's gaze roamed over the painting, then settled on Angel.

"Mine too," Angel said.

Reaching out a hand, she said, "I'm Kinsey Sinclair."

"Angel." The name drew no response from Kinsey. She wondered if "Delaney" would but decided not to try it just yet.

"Are you staying at the resort?" Kinsey asked.

"Yes. I just got in last night." Angel found it hard to talk through the constriction in her throat.

"Welcome to Coeur d'Alene." Kinsey's smile seemed genuine. "I'll leave you to enjoy the gallery. If there's anything I can do or if you have any questions, let me know."

"There is something." The words gushed out before she could

stop them. "Do you know this man?" Angel pulled the photo out of her bag and held it up.

Kinsey stared at the picture, her features turning from surprise to wariness. Returning her gaze to Angel, she asked, "Who are you?"

Angel let herself breathe. "Angel Delaney. I'm . . . I think I may be your sister-in-law."

Kinsey looked away. "That's not possible."

"You met my brother at a summer camp. His best friend was Nick Caldwell."

She licked her lips. "I don't know what to say."

"I need to see him. He's in danger. Nick has been shot."

"I . . ." She shook her head.

"Nick's okay," Angel hastened to say. "But we're concerned that whoever shot him is coming after Luke. Please, help me. Before it's too late."

"I can't . . ."

"We need to talk, Kinsey. Is there any way you can get away from here for a few minutes?"

After a moment, Kinsey nodded. "I'll close up for lunch." She stepped outside and waited for Angel, then locked the door and hung a sign in the window that said she'd be back at 1:00. "Would you like something to eat?"

"Just ate." She folded Luke's photo and stuck it back into her bag.

"Let's walk then."

That was fine with Angel. She didn't want to sit where they might be overheard. They walked to the end of the lobby, then outside and onto a dock, which would eventually take them all the way around the marina.

"How did you find us?" Kinsey asked when they were clear of the building.

Angel gave her the *Reader's Digest* version.

"Thomas has been so worried about Nick."

"You knew?"

She nodded. "You say he's okay?"

"He's fine. Hopefully he'll stay that way. Right now I'm more

134

"We'll do our best." Compassion shone in Warren's eyes. "I just wish Thomas had come to me."

"We talked about it. Especially after what happened to Nick. We were hoping there was no connection, but . . ." She glanced over at Angel. "There has to be."

"Nick survived and identified the bogus gardener as the one who shot him," Angel said. "I'm sure that same guy is the one who was wearing Matt Turlock's badge and the same guy who attacked me at the resort. I took a couple of pictures of him."

Kinsey pulled a package out of her purse. "They're right here."

The chief took them and removed the two photos.

"I was going to fax them to Nick for a positive ID," Angel said.

"We can do that." The chief made a note and looked over at Angel. "I got a call from a Detective Callen Riley, who told me he'd been working on the case until a couple days ago when he handed it over to Detective Downs. I'll be calling Downs when we're finished here. Is there anything else?"

"Unfortunately, yes. I think the 'gardener' also killed a reporter who was taking pictures at the funeral that day. The crime scene investigators are still trying to sort out the mess. I think the killer was looking for incriminating evidence."

"Like a photo placing him at the funeral."

"Exactly. He's good at changing his appearance, but he has this thin, angular face. That's what alerted me to him at the resort."

"You think he may have found Thomas?"

Angel rubbed her forehead. "I don't know. All I know is that Officer Denham and I found a listening device in my purse. I'm assuming it was placed in there before I left Sunset Cove. Just before I came, Nick and I were talking. From some things Luke had told him, Nick suspected he'd be here."

Chief Warren sighed. "Some good detective work on your part. By the way, I heard about your encounter with the bald guy. Sounds like you know how to handle yourself. I'm just sorry he got away from us."

"Not as sorry as I am," Angel said. "The man is dangerous."

"You're still on leave from the police department?"

"Yes."

"And you have a PI license?"

"Yes."

"Hmm. As competent as you seem, I think you need to step aside and let the police handle this investigation."

Angel wasn't certain she could trust the police once they brought Luke in. Would they extradite him to Florida? Would he end up being arrested and brought to trial?

Officer Denham came into the room and in a low voice said something about Sinclair's car.

The chief frowned and looked at the two women. "Thomas's car has been found at the parking lot near the golf course. He was seen leaving with a heavyset man about two hours ago."

Kinsey uttered a sharp cry.

"There's no evidence of foul play at this point," Denham said. "The witness said they seemed friendly."

Heavyset? Angel frowned. "The bald guy who attacked me was definitely not heavyset. Maybe Luke is okay after all."

"But it's not like Thomas to be gone for this long without calling me." Kinsey checked her watch. "I need to pick up Marie. Can I go?"

"Of course." Sam Warren's eyebrows knit in a deep frown. "Ms. Delaney, you're free to leave as well. If either of you hear from Thomas, please let us know."

"You'll keep us posted?" Kinsey asked.

"We'll let you know as soon as we learn anything."

Angel had ridden with Officer Denham to the courthouse and now rode with her sister-in-law to the day care center.

"I'm late. I hope Jennifer won't mind." Kinsey's tone seemed harsh.

"I'm so sorry about all of this." Angel pulled down the visor and dug her sunglasses out of her bag as they drove directly toward the setting sun.

"It's not your fault. Thomas shouldn't have gone to see his father.

He shouldn't have gone to the funeral. He knew how dangerous that man was."

"Getting it out into the open may not be such a bad thing," Angel said. "Luke's been running for years, and leaving us like he did caused more heartache to my family than you can imagine. I'm glad Pop knew Luke was alive when he died."

"I suppose you're right. I'm being selfish, but . . ." Tears gathered in her eyes and dribbled down her cheek before she could reach for the tissues behind her seat. "I'm scared." Kinsey dabbed at her eyes.

"I am too, but I'm not sure there's anything we can do other than pray that the police find the killer before he tries again."

"If he hasn't already." Kinsey took a deep breath, regaining her composure.

"Do you have any idea who Luke might have left the golf course with?" Angel asked. "It doesn't sound like he's in any danger. The guy we're looking for is thin, and Luke left with a heavyset man."

Kinsey shook her head. "I don't know who that could be. Half of the male population is heavyset." She clutched at the tissue in her hand. "I hope you're right about Thomas not being in any danger. But even if you are, what happens to us now? Thomas has no choice but to surrender. We both know what's ahead. He's a suspect in a murder case, and there was talk that he sold out to the Penghetti brothers. No matter what happens, our lives are never going to be the same."

Angel didn't respond. What could she say? They lived in a country where people were supposedly innocent until proven guilty. But the press could have Luke tried and convicted before he even made an appearance in court. Negative publicity like that caused people to lose their jobs and their reputations. Angel knew that firsthand.

Kinsey pulled into a small parking lot and started to get out. "Please don't say anything to Marie about Thomas. I'll just tell her he had to work late. Who knows? Maybe that's true."

Angel nodded. "I'll wait here." With the adrenaline rush long

161

past, she felt exhausted. Had she done the right thing telling the police about Luke?

What's going on, Luke? Where are you? Did you go into hiding again? Who did you leave the golf course with?

Now that she'd found her brother, there were more questions than ever.

Kinsey came out of the house with an adorable little girl at her side. Marie skipped beside Kinsey, smiling as though everything was right with the world. She had Kinsey's eyes, but she reminded Angel of Tim's daughters. No doubt as to their parentage. Kinsey opened the back door, and Marie scrambled in, climbed up into her seat, and fastened her seat belt. "I'm a big girl," she announced to Angel. "Mommy says you're Angel. Are you a real angel or a pretend one?"

Angel twisted more in her seat so she could look at her niece. "My name is Angel. I was born on Christmas Eve and a choir at the hospital where I was born was singing 'Angels We Have Heard on High.' My mother thought that would be a good name for me."

"My mommy says you're my auntie."

Angel glanced at Kinsey and smiled. "That's right. I am."

"I didn't know I had another aunt. Just Auntie Barbara, my mommy's sister."

"Well, I'm your daddy's sister."

"I'm glad." She leaned down, reaching for something in her backpack, and lifted up a work of art. "Want to see what I made for my daddy in art class today?"

"Sure." Angel smiled at the haphazard jumble of colors on a curling piece of paper. "It's beautiful."

"Yes, it is." She tossed it on the floor on top of her pink bag. "I'm an artist, and when I get big, Mommy's going to sell my pictures in the gallery."

Kinsey backed out of the lot and headed down the street, away from the resort. "I thought you might like to have dinner with us," she explained.

"I would. Thank you." Angel suspected that the invitation went beyond dinner. Kinsey didn't want to be alone, which was fine.

Angel wanted to be with her new family and, of course, wanted to be at the house if and when Luke came home.

When Luke hadn't shown up by 9:00, Angel thought it might be best to go back to the resort. She still needed to change rooms and wanted to be settled in before she got too tired to stand up. Kinsey put a drowsy Marie into the car seat and drove the short distance to the resort. She dug into her purse and brought out an envelope. "It's a VIP packet. There's a card inside that allows you to stay in one of our suites at no cost. There's a card for meals too. I've written a note explaining that you're our guest."

Angel thanked her, and thirty minutes later, with the help of a bellman who in no way resembled her attacker, she was wandering through one of the elegant suites on the top floor. "It pays to have brothers in the resort business," she mused.

She clicked on the television set while getting ready for bed. The news came on at 10:00, and she turned up the volume, wondering if anything new had developed. The anchor said nothing about Luke. Nor did they show his photo. Which meant Chief Warren was keeping that part of the case under wraps. They did, however, let their audience know that Matt Turlock, a worker at the resort, was missing. They included a description of the thin bald man who was wanted for questioning in that investigation.

Angel shut off the set and turned out the lights, then sat in a chair beside the window looking out over the lake, wondering how her family could have ended up in such a mess. Regardless of what happened, Angel would have to tell her mother about Luke. She was surprised Ma hadn't seen his picture in the paper or on the news, but then her mother hadn't been all that interested in the news since Frank's death. By the time Luke's picture had hit the paper, Anna was already planning her trip to California. To be on the safe side, Angel had removed that portion of the paper before leaving it on the counter.

Anna Delaney was a strong woman. Even with Frank's illness and eventual death, she'd held on to her faith, knowing God would see her through. Ma would be okay, but how would she take the news that Luke had been alive all these years? She wouldn't be

163

surprised. Ma had often talked about Luke coming home. Angel had no doubt that Anna prayed for Luke every night, as she did for all of her children.

It wasn't right to keep this from her mother, but it didn't seem fair to burden her either. How much could one person take? And what would she say? "Hi, Ma, I found Luke. He's living in Idaho with his wife and their little girl. Only he's missing again, and there's a killer on the loose."

Angel sighed and closed her eyes. She did feel good about one thing, though—telling Callen. She hoped that she hadn't hurt their relationship by not telling him she was coming here. He needed to know he could trust her. Not that she'd lied, she'd just withheld some information.

Angel reached for the phone, needing to bring Nick and Rachael up to date. Figuring Nick would no longer be at the hospital, she called him at home. He picked up on the second ring, and without waiting for more than a hello, Angel told him everything that had transpired.

"I'm sorry, Nick," Angel said when she'd finished. "I had to tell the police everything."

"Don't worry about it. Joe will just chew me out. I'm going to be off for a while, anyway."

"I'm glad it's out in the open, but now with Luke missing, I don't know what to think."

"I hate to say it, Angel, but Luke could have taken off."

"He has a wife and kid now. I can't see him doing that."

"He might if he felt they were in danger. Check his bank account. If there's money missing you can figure he left town. He's changed identities twice that we know of, so he knows how it's done."

Angel swallowed back the painful lump in her throat. "I was so close. I missed him by minutes. Oh, Nick, Kinsey is so nice, and his little girl, Marie." Tears ran freely down her cheeks, and she brushed at them with the sleeve of her pajamas. "She's the cutest little thing. I know Luke wouldn't leave them."

"Maybe not permanently, but like I said, if he knows there's a threat, he may have gotten out of there to protect them. Hang in there, Ange. It'll work out. Trust him. Better yet, trust God."

"Right." She sniffed. "I'm trying to."

"They'll probably call in the feds if he doesn't show up within twenty-four hours."

"Yeah. I'm hoping they don't wait that long. It takes so much time to get anything done. I'm supposed to sit tight, but I don't know if I can."

"I hear you. Of course, you could play a round of golf while you're waiting."

"I could, couldn't I? And I could have Kinsey take a look at their bank account and see if there are any new charges on their credit cards."

"That sounds reasonable."

"How are you feeling, by the way?"

"Not great. I'm wishing I'd stayed in the hospital another day. But don't worry, the guys are taking good care of me. Joe ordered twenty-four hour guards, and they're making sure I have everything I need."

"Good."

"Your mom called today looking for you. I think we're going to need to tell her. She knows something is up."

"How? You didn't say anything, did you?"

"No, but you know your mom. She's got these built-in antennas. Nobody could ever get away with anything around her. Anyway, she's worried 'cause you're not answering at the house."

"She could call my cell."

"She tried. Said you weren't answering that either."

Angel groaned. "Great. The battery must be dead. I forgot to plug it in last night."

"Better call her."

Angel hung up, set her phone in the charger, and went back to the chair and called her aunt's number in California.

Her aunt picked up. "Hi, Angel. I'm so glad you called. Your mother's worried. I told her you were probably out on some hot date, but she wasn't buying it."

"Not a hot date, but I've been busy and I forgot to recharge my cell phone."

"Why don't you come down to visit us too, Angel? We'd love to see you."

"I'd like to see you too, but I can't right now."

When her mother came on the line, Angel apologized for letting her battery go dead. "I tried to call you this afternoon, but you were gone, and I've been too busy to call since."

"Doing what?"

"Just stuff." *Spending time with my sister-in-law and my niece.* Angel wanted so much to tell Anna about Luke and his family, but it was too soon. Ma would want to fly out here, and it just wasn't safe. "So what kind of trouble are you and Aunt Gabby getting into? Have you gone shopping yet?"

"Tomorrow. We're going into the city to hit the outlet stores big time."

"Good. Are you going to buy me something?"

"Of course. When have I ever come back from a trip empty handed?" Ma sounded relaxed and happy.

They talked for a few minutes about Gabby's family, and after about five minutes said their good-byes. Angel phoned Rachael after she hung up with her mother.

"It's about time you called." Rachael sounded upset.

"What's wrong?"

"Plenty. Paul called this afternoon. Angel, something really strange is going on."

"Are they still in Florida?"

"Yes—at their resort. You are not going to believe this. They met with one of the Penghetti brothers."

knew to look for somebody his height and age. My boss told me he'd probably be by himself. I just figured it was him."

Justin sniffed and rubbed his hand under his nose.

"How old are you, Justin?"

"What does that matter?"

"Just curious." Angel blew out a long breath as she examined him. He looked to be in his midtwenties, but his mental state didn't seem to fit with the age. He acted more like a teenager. If he was a drug user, the drugs could've delayed his development. One thing for sure, he wasn't the brightest bulb in the chandelier.

"When you told your boss that you'd found Luke, what did he say?"

"That I should kill both of them."

"Both of them? You told him about Nick too?"

"Yeah. I said that killing wasn't part of the deal, but then he offered me more money. A lot more money."

"How much?"

"Twenty thousand. I got half the money from shooting Nick, 'cause I sent my boss the picture I took."

"But Nick isn't dead."

The Adam's apple shifted again. "I know, but I didn't think the boss would figure it out. I was going to come here and kill Luke and collect the rest of my money and go to Mexico."

"That means you haven't found Luke yet?"

"I was hoping you'd lead me to him, only I got tired of waiting and then you gouged me with those stupid keys."

Angel shook her head, relieved. At least Luke was safe from this creep. "You got shafted, Justin."

"What do you mean?"

"Twenty thousand to kill two men is peanuts. Hit men get at least sixty thousand a head."

He stared at the ground. "Even that's not enough." Glancing in her direction, he asked, "What's going to happen now?"

"Depends on how well you cooperate with the police." She folded her arms and took a step toward him. "What happened to Faith Carlson?"

"Who?"

183

"The reporter?"

"What reporter?"

Angel sighed. "Come on, Justin, you know who I mean. The woman who was taking pictures at my father's funeral. The one I found dead in her house."

He looked out at the lake. "I—I didn't mean to kill her. I just broke into her house to get the pictures she took of me. Not of me exactly, but she aimed the camera in my direction. I was just gonna take the pictures and get out of there, but there were too many, and she came home while I was looking around. I didn't know what to do so I wrapped a telephone cord around her neck, and then I pushed her on the floor and ran."

Angel felt sick and rested her hand on her stomach, working to regain some objectivity and wondering how much more damage the guy had done. "Did you get the pictures?"

"I couldn't find them, but I figured it would be okay 'cause I look different now."

If he didn't have the pictures, then where were they? She rubbed her forehead. "Did you get rid of anyone else, Justin?"

"Can't we just go now?"

"What about Kinsey Sinclair?"

"I didn't do nothin' to her. I was just saying that to make you cooperate."

"What about Matt, the guy whose clothes and ID you stole? What happened to him?"

Justin chewed on a fingernail. "You ask too many questions."

"Let me tell you something, Justin. Your boss isn't going to be too happy when he finds out that you didn't actually kill Nick. Which means you're a dead man if and when he gets hold of you. I might be able to help you stay alive, but you're going to have to do exactly what I say. Where's Matthew Turlock?"

"At the resort."

"Where? The resort is a big place. What did you do with him?"

"Maybe I'll tell the cops. You taking me in?"

So that was it. He didn't want to tell her everything in case she changed her mind and decided to leave him there or kill him. "I said I was."

"Maybe I'll tell you more if you let me go," Justin said.

"Believe me, your chances of survival are a lot better with the police than with your boss." She kicked the bottom of his tennis shoe. "Where is Matt?"

He scowled. "Figure it out yourself."

"Fine. Get up." She untied his feet. "We're going back to the marina. On the way I'm calling the police and having them meet us at the dock. Then you're going to tell them what you told me. And I'd strongly advise you to tell them what you've done with Matt Turlock."

Justin seemed to have lost his starch in his battle with the lake. He didn't argue, nor did he try to get away when she instructed him to get into the boat. To be on the safe side, she tied him up in the cabin before going back out to release the craft and get it out into deeper water. Half an hour later, she pulled up to the outside dock, where two police officers were waiting.

"Don't ask," she said when Officer Denham looked from her to Justin, then back again, no doubt taking in the still-damp clothes and her stringy hair. "Just keep this guy on ice until I can get changed and get down to the station."

"Sure."

"By the way, he told me Matt was here at the hotel. Have you located him yet?"

"No luck."

"He knows where Matt is, but for some reason he isn't telling."

Denham gave her a hand out of the boat.

"And my brother?"

"Sorry, we haven't found him either."

Angel thought she saw Justin's mouth, now devoid of lipstick, turn up at the corner. Maybe he wasn't as dumb as he seemed. She had a hunch he was using Matt's whereabouts as a trump card to plea-bargain. And maybe he'd gotten to Luke after all. She wished now she'd spent more time getting answers out of him.

After leaving Justin Moore in Officer Denham's capable hands, Angel jogged back along the dock and into the resort, briefly peeking into the gallery to make sure Kinsey was all right. She was with a customer. At least Justin had told Angel the truth on that score.

Twenty minutes later, Angel had showered and was wearing jeans and a burgundy turtleneck and a warm jacket. All that time in cold, wet clothes had left her chilled to the bone.

She walked past the gallery and noticed Kinsey talking to the same person. Kinsey halted the conversation and came to the store's entrance. "Any news about Thomas?"

Angel shook her head. "I take it you haven't heard from him either?"

"No. I'm going to finish up with my client and pick up Marie." Tears slipped through despite her struggle to retain her composure. "Where could he be? I hate to think the worst, but I'm . . ."

"I know, but we need to keep thinking positively. I have to go down to the police station for a while, then I'll come by the house. We need to talk."

Kinsey nodded, and Angel instinctively wrapped her arms around the woman. Though she'd only known Kinsey for two days, they were family, and the connection to Luke corded them together. "We'll find him," Angel said, feeling like she'd just stolen the lines from her mother. "Just keep praying."

Ma should be here. You're not being fair to her by leaving her out. Eventually she would have to call Ma. But not yet.

The valet brought Angel's Corvette around, and within five minutes she had parked and was walking into the police station.

"Hello, Angel," a familiar voice greeted her as she stepped inside.

THIRTY-SEVEN

_____

Callen!" She didn't know whether to be annoyed or pleased. Pleased, she decided as she walked into his arms and felt them wrap her in his strength. Definitely pleased.

"What are you doing here?" She pulled away and looked into his dark eyes. "I mean, I'm glad to see you, but what about your meetings and your talk?"

"I had my final presentation this morning and caught the first flight out. I talked to my supervisor, and I'm back on the case. Detective Downs is still tied up with the reporter's death. He finally found the photos she'd taken at the funeral."

"At her house?"

He shook his head. "They were in the mailbox."

"No wonder Justin didn't find them. Did Detective Downs send them here?"

"Justin?"

"Long story. First tell me about the photos."

"I've already looked through them. There are a number of people I don't recognize, thought maybe you'd like to have a look."

"I would." She hesitated. "First, though, I need to give my statement to these guys. I caught the creep who tried to kill Nick. He's a piece of work. He killed the reporter too—strangled her with an electric cord."

187

"You caught him?" Callen raised an eyebrow, looking none too pleased.

"After he caught me." She smiled. "Like I said, it's a long story, and I'm only going to tell it once, so you'd better come with me."

The interview room was stark and filled with a table and several chairs. Angel sat down in the chair the chief pulled out for her. Another officer had a tape recorder set up, ready and waiting.

Chief Warren rested his hands on the table. "Would you like some coffee or a soft drink?"

"How about an iced vanilla latte?" she teased, hoping to lighten the somber mood.

Warren didn't seem to appreciate the humor.

"Seriously, some regular coffee is fine."

"Never let it be said that we don't treat our visitors well," the chief responded. "Jake, run over to the coffee shop and get the lady an iced vanilla latte." He accentuated the last words, leaving no doubt as to his disapproval of her. Callen leaned against the wall, arms folded, taking it all in. Probably wondering what the antagonism was all about.

She stifled her growing annoyance. Okay, so maybe she had overstepped her boundaries. Still, he should be thankful she'd brought the guy in rather than leaving them with another crime to deal with—her murder.

There must have been an espresso place right next door because her latte appeared in less than five minutes, about the time it took to introduce Callen to the others and get the small talk over with.

After taking several sips of her drink, Angel indicated her readiness to begin the interview. Speaking into the microphone, she gave her account of the abduction and how she was able to gain the upper hand. "The problem is, he wouldn't tell me what he'd done with Matthew. Did you get anything out of him?"

The chief, who'd been quiet while she spoke, got out of his chair and moved toward her. "We haven't officially interrogated him. Wanted to get your statement first. We have the key to the motel room where he was staying, though. My officers are going through it right now."

"What about his car? He must have followed me here from Sunset Cove, so we're probably looking for Oregon plates."

The chief nodded. "We have a couple guys going over the parking garage at the resort and the adjoining parking areas."

Callen cleared his throat. "When you find his car, I'd have a look in the trunk."

"Intuition, detective?" the chief wondered.

"Experience."

"Thanks. I'm sure we'd have gotten to that eventually." The chief's sarcastic tone instigated an unkind look from Callen. Callen was encroaching on the chief's territory, and the chief didn't like it. He wasn't too thrilled about learning of Luke's deception either, so all the way around the Delaneys had gotten his dander up.

"Since you seem to have gotten more out of him than we have, can you tell us if Moore gave you any indication of what might have happened to your brother?" the chief asked.

"He said he hadn't seen him. Anyway, he doesn't fit the description of the guy who left the clubhouse with Luke. But that doesn't mean he's telling the truth. Luke may have left with a guy he knew, but suppose Justin got to him later?" Angel suggested they interview people at Luke's favorite haunts.

"We could be dealing with more than one guy here," Callen said. "Moore might have a partner."

"At least two," Angel said. "Justin has a boss in Florida, and I'm betting that boss is one of the Penghetti brothers." She told Callen and the chief the story she'd gotten from Rachael about Bobby and Bernard Penghetti interviewing her twin brothers.

"Unbelievable." The chief threw up his hands. "What part of 'stay out of this' don't you people understand?"

Angel bristled at his tone. "I'm cooperating with you here, Chief. I'm trying to keep you informed of everything that's happened. I can't help it if Justin decided to abduct me. And I certainly didn't have anything to do with the mob interviewing my brothers. Luke is in trouble, and I'm having a hard time trying to figure out who the bad guys are."

Callen smiled. "You're wasting your breath telling Angel to

189

butt out, Chief. Tell you what. I'll take her off your hands and out of your hair."

"Hey!" Angel fumed. "What's that supposed to mean?"

Callen tossed her a "stifle yourself" look and winked at her. Angel wasn't certain what Callen meant by that last comment, but his wink silenced her. She took it to mean that he intended to run interference between her and the chief, which was probably a good thing.

"Since this all started in Oregon," Callen said, "why don't you give me the authority to run my investigation here." Callen turned back to the chief. "I'll need one or two of your guys to work with me, make arrests, and be the affiant on any warrants. And I'll need a letter of permission from your agency."

Chief Warren looked from Callen to Angel. "All right, but Ms. Delaney, try to stay out of trouble. You got lucky with Mr. Moore."

"Luck had little to do with it, Chief." Callen assured him. "Angel has been in law enforcement for years. She's very good at what she does. If anyone is lucky, it's you. Hard to say how long it would have taken to bring the guy in if Angel hadn't been next on his list."

His attitude softened a bit. "I suppose that's one way to look at it."

Seeing an opening, Angel asked about the pictures that had been found in Faith Carlson's mailbox. "Why were they in the mailbox, Callen? Do we know?"

Callen nodded. "According to a friend of hers, Faith was an amateur photographer and processed a lot of her work. She didn't trust herself with the important stuff—like photos she planned to use in the newspaper. Those she'd send out to be processed professionally. A company in Portland did the work and mailed them back to her. These photos were in her mailbox, so we were able to take them in as evidence."

Angel watched as a uniformed female officer, introduced as Officer Colbert, came in and systematically placed one photo on top of another. "Just tell me if anything or anyone stands out to you."

Ma would appreciate these, Angel thought, reliving the painful service. It felt odd looking at herself and the rest of the family from someone else's eyes. She blinked back tears, willing herself not to cry.

"Wait!" She picked up one of the photos, examining it more closely. "There he is." Angel pointed to the gardener. "That's Justin."

The chief looked at the picture. "I can see why you wouldn't have recognized him. Except for the thinness in his face, he looks like a completely different person now. I'll have our lab people compare this to the photos you gave us of the bald guy."

"I'm just glad he slipped up at the resort or I might not have noticed him at all." She shuddered. "The man is stupid but dangerous."

Colbert made a note and set the photo aside and went on to the next.

Angel pointed out Luke, who was standing alone near a large maple. Another picture revealed a heavyset man wearing dark glasses and a suit and tie, whom Angel didn't recognize. She hadn't noticed him at the funeral, probably because he blended in with the others and stood close to friends and other family members, just behind Aunt Gabby and her husband. Middle aged, heavyset. She thought about the description that Marty at the golf course had given her. "This guy." Angel looked up at Callen. "Do you know him?"

"No. He was on my list to ask you about."

"I don't remember seeing him before now. He fits the description of the guy Luke left the golf course with."

"Him and about half the men at the resort. Middle aged and heavyset. That's me." The chief sighed and ran a hand through his graying hair. "Anyone else?"

Angel looked over the photos again and picked out several other men she didn't know.

"We'll get enlargements of the people you pointed out to us. I'll have one of our officers take the photos out to the club. See if Marty recognizes any of them."

Angel wanted to be the one to do that but kept her mouth shut.

191

"I'd like a copy of the photos as well," Callen said.

Officer Colbert agreed. "I'll get these scanned and printed right away." She took the photos and hurried out of the room.

Officer Denham came in and whispered something to the chief.

The chief frowned. His hands moved down to grip the back of the chair. "We found the Turlock kid."

Angel's heart sank. She knew before he told them that the news wasn't good.

"You were right, Detective Riley. Matthew was in the trunk of Justin Moore's rental car. He's dead."

Angel picked up her drink and swished it around, the swirling ice making far too much noise in the silent room.

"Denham, I'll leave it to you to inform the family," Chief Warren said. "And since you're familiar with the case, I'd like you to work with Detective Riley."

"Yes, sir." Officer Denham nodded, his gaze capturing Angel's. "At least you caught the guy who did it. The family will appreciate knowing that."

"I just wish I'd known he was following me. Maybe I could have prevented Matt's death." Angel felt an overwhelming sense of responsibility. "I was trained to notice things like that."

Callen came over to stand behind her chair, his hands settling on her shoulders. "If we're done here, Chief, I'd like to get going."

"Just one thing." The chief rested his hands on his hips, drawing attention to his thick waist. "I'm releasing a photo of Luke to the television station to let people know he's missing. Maybe we'll get lucky. I wish I hadn't automatically decided the man in the photo wasn't Thomas. If I'd taken him in, he might still be . . . with us."

Angel reached out and touched the back of his hand. "Luke is your friend, and you couldn't have known about his past. No matter how bad this looks, I have to keep thinking Luke is okay."

"All this wishing we'd done things differently isn't going to change the past," Callen said. "In order to get anywhere with this investigation, we're going to have to take a closer look at what

ing money and power do not always equal corruption. Take your brothers, for example; they have a great deal of money. They are powerful men, but they are honest as well, don't you agree?"

"Of course, but why would the state bring charges against you if there wasn't some truth in what my sources have told me?"

"You ask good questions, Angel." He took a sip of his merlot. "Years ago, our reputation was tarnished when one of my cousins used his wealth to purchase land in Colombia and build a large operation involving drugs there. But Leonardo was caught and killed by the DEA."

"When was that?"

"Twenty years ago, I'm sure. My father and uncle can't watch every aspect of the family business. If they hear of a problem, they deal with it immediately. Stanton was a problem."

"So you had him killed and set it up so Luke was blamed."

"No." Bernie sighed. "We fired him and fully cooperated with the police in his arrest."

"I'd sure like to know what Stanton had to say about you that was so condemning."

"Lies. I do have access to the transcripts from the trial up until the charges were dropped."

"I'd like to see them."

"How is your mother, Angel?" Bernie asked out of the blue. "This situation with her husband and son must be very hard on her."

Why was he asking about her mother? Was his question a threat under the guise of caring? But Anna was safe at Aunt Gabby's, wasn't she? No one outside the family and Rachael knew where Anna had gone. Although that wasn't quite true. Had the Penghettis planted the listening device? "She's coping. Grieving."

Angel suddenly realized that Anna Delaney might have another loss to deal with. A daughter. And then there was the finding and losing of Luke a second time. She wondered if Callen had notified Anna that Angel had been taken for a ride by a mobster. Angel hoped not. On the other hand, Ma needed to know what was going on. Angel wished she'd confided in her early on. Now it might be too late.

She brought her attention back to her hosts. Were Bernie and Dan rocking her into complacency? If she worked with them to find Luke, what would happen to her? As pleasant as they could be, she couldn't trust anything they said, and more importantly, she needed to remain an asset to them.

The entire situation here at the condo with Bernard Penghetti and Dan seemed surreal. She wouldn't have been at all surprised to learn that she'd dreamed up the whole thing.

After they'd eaten, she sat down at the computer again with Bernie, who brought up several files he'd obtained on the trial and on the DA. These he printed off so Angel could read them more thoroughly later on. Once he'd given the print command, he announced that he was tired and would be going to bed.

"What am I supposed to do for pajamas and stuff?" Angel asked him. "And where am I supposed to sleep?"

"There's a second bedroom upstairs." Bernie stopped on the landing. "While we were working on the computer, Dan picked up some things at the general store. I'm sure you'll find enough to get by."

Alone in the condo with two men. The realization that this could be a very dangerous situation churned up the contents of her stomach, nearly causing her to flee to the bathroom.

"Don't worry, kid," Dan said. "You're safe with us."

Angel didn't like Dan buying her things, and she especially didn't like him knowing what she was thinking. "I wasn't worried." She turned back to the computer and clicked on the mailbox. There was a note for Bernie from his wife telling him she missed him and that Jimmy had had a good day. She went to her server's website and clicked on her own mail.

The first email was from Rachael. Apparently Callen had told her about Angel's plan to rescue Kinsey and Marie. *"You're crazy, Angel. Please, please do not trust these people. They are dangerous!!!!"*

Another message had come in from Callen saying he'd gone to the PD and was waiting for the guard to bring Justin out to talk with him. He explained that he'd lost the connection with her cell and had gone around to the back of the house to get closer. By the time he got into place, he heard the car start up and take off. Without her keys, he'd had to wait for a patrol car, and by then it was too late. He too warned her not to trust Penghetti.

Annoyance crept in. Didn't he and Rachael realize that she wasn't dumb? Of course she had told them she was being taken care of—partly because she hadn't wanted them to worry, but mostly because she hadn't wanted to write something that Bernie or Dan might see. She deleted the messages and glanced over her shoulder. Dan was still in the kitchen, and Angel noticed the car keys on the counter. She averted her eyes before Dan could catch her looking at them.

"Well, guess I'll get started on my reading." She stretched and yawned.

Dan nodded and continued to load the dishwasher. "Good night."

"Night." Angel took the thick sheaf of paper up to the bedroom and set it on the nightstand. Slipping off her shoes, she padded across the plush beige carpet into the private bath. While brushing her teeth with a new brush and toothpaste, she thought about her best means of escape. It seemed simple enough: just wait until both men were asleep, sneak downstairs, take the keys, and leave. She hadn't noticed an alarm system, so her plan should work—if she could get by Dan. If he awoke when she attempted her getaway, she'd just tell him she was thirsty and wanted a drink of water.

Angel played the escape scene over and over in her mind, wondering how long it would take for Dan to fall asleep. She eyed the pajamas laid out on the bed and opted to stay dressed, at least for now. At midnight, she'd go downstairs and reevaluate. In the meantime she'd read.

Angel had had only a surface look at the case in which Luke had been involved. Rachael's information had given her a bit more background on the case, but these documents seemed to cover everything. There were articles as well as court documents and testimonies. The charges against the Penghetti brothers included graft, fraud, drug dealing, and even murder. The witness was expected to testify to being present while one of their dealers, a young Latino, was killed by Bobby and Rick Penghetti. The DA's office had apparently been after the brothers for a long time, but for various reasons, lack of evidence being one of them, the brothers were never formally charged. On this occasion, the DA was quoted as saying: "This time the charges will stick." Angel wondered why everything lay so heavily on one witness.

Angel read through the details, thinking Bernie may not have been entirely wrong in thinking the DA was somehow responsible. What if the witness had changed his mind and decided to tell the court that the DA had bribed him? That would certainly be motive for murder. DA wants a conviction. He hires the witness. Witness changes his mind. DA hires a hit.

The scenario was far-fetched but almost as believable as the Penghetti brothers hiring the hit. The media blamed the Penghetti brothers, and who could argue with their reasoning? Without the witness, the brothers would go free. According to the DA's office, however, only Luke and the DA knew where the witness and guard were staying. How had the killer found them? Of course, information could easily be bought. Perhaps the brothers had a spy at the hotel who provided them with the information. Or maybe they knew someone at the DA's office.

In an attached note, Angel found the DA's name and address, making note of the fact that he had left his job shortly after the shooting incident. Which corresponded with what Rachael had told her. He was also living very well, she noted, as an attorney in private practice.

Angel set the stack of papers aside and rubbed her blurry eyes. She wanted to go home, sit out on her deck, and watch the stars. Discouragement washed over her like the waves on the ocean. Would she ever find Luke? And if she or the authorities did find him, would he be alive? The Penghetti brothers wanted Luke, and whoever Justin had been working for wanted him too. Were they the same people? Justin was too young to have been the original hit man, so was that person after Luke as well? Did Luke have some kind of information that could incriminate all of them? Who had gotten to Luke first? Who had hired Justin? Far too many questions. She needed to talk to Callen. He would have shown the photo to Justin by now. Had he emailed her back? Could she check the computer?

When Angel made her way downstairs, it was nearly midnight. Dan was lying on the couch and appeared to be asleep. The computer was closed, and Angel toyed with the idea of turning it on. Dan would undoubtedly wake up when it came on and chimed its welcome.

In the dim light she could see the keys still sitting on the counter. She went back into the bedroom to retrieve her bag but couldn't find it; then she realized she'd left it in the living room near the computer. She put on her shoes and crept down the stairs and crossed the room to the computer. The purse wasn't there. Had Dan moved it?

You don't have time to search for it now. To make certain Dan was asleep, she went into the kitchen, plucking the keys off the counter and tucking them into her pocket as she went by. She took down a glass, filled it with water, drank most of the water, and set the glass down. Dan hadn't stirred and was softly snoring.

Taking several deep breaths to calm her fragile nerves, Angel slipped outside and down the concrete steps into the garage. She made her way to the limo and clicked the remote to unlock the door. It gave its annoying honk, and Angel's breath caught and held. She slipped inside and inserted the key, twisting it as she watched the stairs. Apparently no one had heard. Moments later, she was on the main road heading back to Coeur d'Alene.

On the outskirts of town, she passed a patrol car, and moments later she saw that the car was following her, lights flashing.

The stop didn't surprise her. Callen had probably alerted the authorities to be on the lookout for the vehicle. She pulled over.

"May I see your driver's license and registration please?" the sheriff's deputy said when he arrived at her window.

"I don't have my license. I was sort of abducted and I escaped, but I couldn't find my bag." She leaned over and popped the button on the glove box and pulled out the rental agreement. "It's a rental car."

"You're driving without a license?"

"Yes, but I just explained why." She handed him the papers.

"It's rented to Bernard Penghetti or Dan something." She rubbed her forehead as he looked over the forms. He wasn't buying her story, she could tell. "Look, my name is Angel Delaney. I'm a cop. If you don't believe me, you can call Detective Callen Riley." She gave him Callen's cell number. "Or call the police department in Coeur d'Alene. They'll know who I am."

"Step out of the car." His voice was stern.

"Officer, please. We're wasting valuable time here."

"Out of the car, slowly."

Angel complied. "Please, just call the police department."

He had her lean against the car and quickly patted her down.

"I'm not armed. I'm just trying to get into town."

"Save it." He cuffed her, then ushered her into the backseat of his patrol car.

"You're taking me in?" She didn't especially like the idea of being hauled into jail, but at least there she'd be able to get someone to corroborate her story. "But what about the car?"

"I'll take care of it."

The officer didn't believe a word she'd said, and she didn't really blame him. If she had stopped someone without a license driving a vehicle rented to someone else, she doubted she'd believe them either. The officer needed to verify that she was who she said she was. No matter, she'd soon be in town calling Callen to come get her. She leaned back, sighing in relief.

The officer removed the keys from the limo and locked it up, leaving it at the side of the rode. Once inside his own vehicle, he called for a tow. Bernie and Dan would not be happy to discover they'd been left without a car.

The officer drove a short distance on the two-lane highway toward town, then at a pullout made a U-turn and headed back in the direction they'd just come.

"What's going on? Where are we going?" She spotted the limo parked on the opposite side of the road. Unbelievable. He was taking her back to Penghetti.

FORTY-TWO

The officer eyed her in the rearview mirror. "Just cool your jets, Miss Penghetti. You're lucky I'm taking you back to your uncle and not to jail. He said he didn't want to press charges."

"My uncle? You talked to him?" Angel leaned back. *Great. This is just great. The guy doesn't believe a word I said, and I don't have ID to prove it.* "I suppose he told you I'd say I'd been abducted and that I'd give you a phony name."

"Which is exactly what you did."

"I am Angel Delaney. Please, just call the Coeur d'Alene PD."

He smiled. "I already did, ma'am. They never heard of you."

"How can that be?" Angel sucked in a sharp breath. "Please don't take me back to the condo. They'll kill me."

He chuckled. "You sound like my daughter. I doubt you have anything to be afraid of, except maybe being grounded. Mr. Penghetti seems like a nice guy."

"Grounded? Did he tell you how old I am?"

"Yeah. Seventeen going on thirty, which looks about right."

She probably did look like a teenager. Her small stature and unruly curls had most people questioning her age. "How much did he pay you to bring me back?"

"I don't accept money." He frowned. "Just doing my job."

encouraged Dr. Hathaway and Cade to transfer Luke to the car so he could get medical help as soon as possible. The sooner Ethan could get Luke to the hospital, the sooner he'd contact Callen and get him out here. She'd feel a hundred times better if she could even the odds.

When they could no longer see the red Camry, Cade ambled back to the cabin. He stopped before going inside and looked back at Angel. "They'll be a while. Want to do a little fishing?"

FORTY-SIX

Never—not even in her wildest imagination—did Angel think she'd be sitting in a boat in the middle of a cool, clear Idaho lake, watching the wildlife and catching fish with a murderer. Yet being here with Cade seemed oddly peaceful.

A doe and a buck came down to the water to drink and didn't seem to mind sharing with the humans. Water lapped gently against the boat while Angel put another worm on the hook and dropped in her line. "My father would've loved it here."

"Mine as well."

Angel hesitated before asking her question. "How did you and Ethan take such different paths in life?"

"You mean how did we end up on opposite sides of the law? My father was murdered when I was just ten and Ethan twelve. Our mother died soon after, and we were placed in the system and adopted out to different families. Ethan handled things differently than me. He took the losses in stride and became attached to his adopted parents. I became angry and rebelled. Ethan went to law school, graduated with honors. I graduated with a business degree and became a stockbroker who dabbled in . . . other things."

"Killing people." As strange as it seemed, Angel found Cade easy to talk to, and that bothered her.

"On occasion." He lifted his pole and set it down again. "Most of the time, the killings were made to look like accidents. At first

I fancied myself a vigilante of sorts. I suppose psychiatrists would say I was avenging my father's death. Most of my victims, if you could call them that, were bad guys who had beaten the system. I'm quite certain some of my clients were actually police officers who wanted to see justice done."

"Did they know who you were?"

"No. There were always safeguards. I became an expert in disguises and had a number of aliases."

"And Ethan knew about this?"

He shook his head. "We lost touch for a while, and by the time I found him again, I was efficiently leading a double life."

"Do you have other family?" Angel took a sip of diet cola she'd brought along.

"I never married. Relationships make you too vulnerable, and I had to be ready to move on at a moment's notice."

"What made you decide to give it up?"

"Age. Conscience. I felt justified in what I was doing, and now . . . let's just say my worldview has changed considerably—partly because of your brother."

"Luke?"

"Tim. I followed you when you went to church and heard his sermon on salvation."

"You really don't know who hired you to kill Luke?"

"My client had safeguards, and I couldn't trace him."

The sound of tires crunching on gravel and the purring of a car's engine penetrated the silence, and Angel glanced back toward the cabin. Cade heard it as well. "Looks like we have company," he said.

"It's too soon for Ethan to be back."

Angel spotted the black limousine through the trees as it turned into the driveway. Two men emerged from the car. Dan and Bernie. "That's Bernie Penghetti and his bodyguard."

Cade reeled in his line and set the pole in the boat, then picked up the oars. "We'd better head for cover. I don't know how they managed to find us, but I doubt they're out for a joyride."

Angel reeled in her line as well. The men had disappeared from

245

sight, no doubt checking out the cabin. When they realized it was empty, would they think to look out on the lake?

Cade's powerful strokes pulled them off to the side, and within seconds they were hidden from Bernie and Dan's view.

"What are we going to do?" Angel's mind raced with possibilities. "Ethan and Callen will be here soon."

"How could they have known about the cabin?" Cade frowned and settled the oars in the boat as they touched the shoreline.

Angel frowned. "I'll bet Bernie planted some kind of tracking device or a GPS in my purse or in my pocket. I didn't even think to check." She groaned. "How could I be such an idiot?" The purse was in the cabin along with Cade's gun. Would Bernie and Dan wait for someone to show up? Or would they leave when they found the cabin empty?

"Perhaps we can get to the road and warn Ethan before he gets to the cabin." Cade peered into the woods.

"Good idea." They'd rowed to the west of the cabin. The forest and brush would be hard to navigate. "How far is the road from here?"

"Probably half a mile, no more. If we go straight ahead, we should come to it."

"All right, then, let's go." Angel began jogging, and Cade followed, but within a few feet he faded back. "Can't run," he gasped. "Pain in my chest. Go ahead. I'll wait for you by the boat."

Angel hesitated. "Are you sure? I . . ."

"Go. I'll be okay if I rest." He pulled at the chain around his neck, which looked like it held a vial of nitroglycerine tablets.

Angel turned and ran ahead, hoping she wouldn't have to wait long for Callen and Ethan, and hoping Cade would be all right. It seemed strange to be praying for the life of a killer, but God help her, she actually liked the man. Cade had chosen to let Luke go free in that hotel room in Florida. That had to count for something.

She made it to the road in six minutes—fast for the conditions, but not fast enough. The Camry and a patrol car passed just as she came out of the woods.

Angel sprinted after the car, waving. With the cloud of dust following them, she doubted they'd see her. The driveway came up far more quickly than she expected. When she arrived at the cabin, she could see that Callen and Officer Denham had their guns drawn. Bernie and Dan were standing on the porch, looking confused. Ethan and another man got out of the backseat.

Angel slowed and came up beside Callen. "I tried to warn you that they were here."

"I saw their limo just as I was turning in." He turned to Officer Denham. "Go ahead and cuff them."

"Where's Cade?" Ethan asked.

"In the woods. I can take you to him. But first, I think we need to deal with Penghetti and his bodyguard."

"What did I tell you?" The man from the backseat stood with his hands on his hips. Angel didn't need an introduction. She recognized Alton Delong from the pictures on the Internet. Her gaze darted back to Callen. "What's he doing here?"

"Mr. Delong flew in from Florida yesterday." Callen motioned to Angel. "Alton Delong, this is Angel Delaney."

"Pleased to meet you, Angel. I can't tell you how happy I am that your brother is safe."

"You talked to him?"

"Yes. I was fortunate enough to be chatting with Detective Riley here when Ethan brought him in. I thought it appropriate to come along when Callen arrested the man responsible for killing Stanton and the guard."

Callen must have seen the questioning look in her eyes. "Mr. Delong had nothing to do with this, Angel. Bernie was leading you down a rabbit trail. We traced Justin's cell phone to Richard Penghetti. Rick must have hired Justin and given him the phone, since the phone is registered to him. I'm thinking he sent his nephew out here to finish the job."

Angel looked back at Alton, whose face shone with the glow of victory. "So the investigation is over. Just like that." She looked over to where Bernie and Dan stood handcuffed. "I wouldn't have thought Bernie and Dan would give up without a fight."

"There's been a grievous mistake here, Angel," Bernie called out to her. "Please, listen to me."

"Right. What are you doing out here, anyway? How did you know to come here?"

"While you were asleep, I had Dan sew a tracking device into your bag. I apologize, but I wanted to know if and when you found Luke."

"So you could kill him?"

"Of course not."

"Save the chatter for later," Callen said. "Officer Denham, read them their rights."

"We haven't done anything wrong," Bernie insisted.

Callen put both men in the back of Denham's patrol car and called for assistance. He'd given orders to have the sheriff and several deputies on standby.

"Where did you say Cade was?" Callen asked.

She told him about having to leave Cade in the woods. When additional officers came to transport Bernie and Dan into town, Angel took Callen and Officer Denham to where she'd left Cade. They walked along the lake but couldn't find the boat. After more than an hour of searching, Angel came to the conclusion she'd been outwitted. "He's gone. And knowing Cade, you'll probably never find him."

"Don't be too sure." Callen put out an APB and said he wanted to expand the search along the lake.

Angel opted to go back into town with Ethan and the DA so she could see Luke. Part of her hoped Cade had gotten away and part of her wanted him in prison. She still puzzled over the outcome of the investigation, thinking something just didn't seem right. She sat in the backseat, listening to Delong and Hathaway discussing old times.

"Finally," Alton said, "Richard Penghetti will be going to jail. I've waited a long time for this."

"I'm glad for you, Alton," Ethan said. "I find it very strange, however, that Rick Penghetti would purchase a set of cell phones in his own name and give one to the kid he hired to kill Luke. I'd have thought him smarter than that."

Angel sat up straighter and caught the professor's gaze in the rearview mirror. "I wondered about that too," she said.

"I see your point, but you need to realize that Rick is getting up there in years," Delong said. "It may not have occurred to him that he'd ever get caught. I suspect he was planning to do away with Justin and take the cell phone back. He probably didn't think it would ever end up with the police."

"Do you think Rick Penghetti had Justin killed?" Angel asked.

"No doubt about it. That's how these guys operate. It's hard to trace anything back to them, but we've done it."

The professor sighed. "Well, I'm glad it's over. I have to admit, though, for a while, I thought you might have been the one to hire the hit man."

"Me? Why on earth would I do that?"

"Well, you did have reason to hate Rick Penghetti."

Angel leaned back, wondering where the professor was heading. She and Rachael had talked about Delong's dedication and how he might have been overzealous. Callen needed to hear this, but calling him at this point might be a mistake.

Ethan cleared his throat. "I seem to remember an accident many years ago—you lost your daughter, right?"

"What does that have to do with anything?"

Angel held her breath.

"As I recall, a young man by the name of Richard Penghetti had been drinking and ran a red light the night your little girl died. He was tried and convicted of vehicular manslaughter, but served no jail time. That must have infuriated you."

So Alton Delong had motive. Angel didn't like Alton Delong's arrogant attitude. And Ethan had a point. If she were Richard Penghetti, there was no way she'd leave herself vulnerable by putting her own name on a cell phone specifically set up to converse with a hit man. And if Richard was the ultimate bad guy Delong made him out to be, why hire a loser like Justin Moore to do his dirty work? He had family who could do that sort of work for him.

"Of course it infuriated me," Alton said, "but you have it all wrong. I wanted to get back at Rick, yes, but not illegally. That family is evil. I just wanted to see justice done."

"There is no justice when you take the law into your own hands, Alton."

"That's a lecture you should have saved for your brother."

Ethan nodded. "My opportunity came too late, I'm afraid."

"What happens now?" Angel asked.

"The police will question Penghetti and his friend, but won't have much luck," Alton answered. "They'll bring in their attorneys and be on the street before the day is over. But with the cell phone connection, we'll be able to bring charges up against Richard for the murders of Nick Caldwell, Faith Carlson, and Justin Moore."

"It's all circumstantial evidence." Ethan said.

"That may be, but the jury will convict."

Angel was still hung up on Alton's explanation. Nick's murder? And how did he know about Justin? How much had Callen told him? "How did you know about Justin and Nick?"

"Detective Riley filled me in on the case on the way out here."

The professor's look of surprise told her what she already knew. Alton Delong had just dug his own grave, and unfortunately, he knew it.

"Stop the car." Delong drew a gun and pointed it at the professor's head.

Ethan glanced at her in the rearview mirror as if asking, *What now?*

"Do as he says." Angel had no idea what Delong would do or what he might be capable of.

Ethan pulled off the highway, and Alton told them to get out. He yelled at Angel to get into the driver's seat. "You're going to be my insurance until I can get out of the vicinity."

"And if I refuse?"

"Then I put a bullet in the professor's head."

Angel eased in behind the wheel while Delong climbed into the passenger seat. Before closing the door, he fired off a shot, striking Ethan in the chest.

"No!" Like a tennis player with a killer backhand, Angel slammed her fist into Alton's face. Pain shot up her arm.

250

He screamed and brought his right hand up. She took advantage of his confusion and grabbed for his gun with both hands. Not about to give it up, he dove out of the car, bringing Angel with him. She lay on top of him, straddling his waist and still holding tight to the gun.

Blood spurted from his nose, and he coughed, splattering them both. He loosened his grip, and Angel wrenched the gun from his grasp, then stuck the barrel into his ribs. "Don't move." She used the sleeve of her jacket to wipe the blood from her face.

Pushing herself off him, she yelled, "On your stomach, stretch your arms up in front of you where I can see them. Now!"

Delong whimpered. "I had them. I had Penghetti where he belongs. You idiot. Do you know how much damage you've caused?"

"Looks like I have you where you belong." Keeping the weapon aimed at Delong, she pulled her cell from her pocket and dialed 911, asking the operator to contact Callen and Chief Warren and to send an ambulance. Callen was still at the cabin, which was only about five miles away. As she spoke she backed over to Ethan. His tanned face had already turned a pasty shade of gray. The blood pulsing from his chest told her he wouldn't make it. Still, she dropped the phone and pressed her free hand to his wound in an attempt to stop the bleeding. "Stay with me, Ethan."

"I'm sorry." He covered her hand with hers. There was nothing more she could do. She stood and wiped her bloody hand on her jacket.

Angel didn't have to wait long for help. Callen and Brad Denham arrived first. Callen took one look at Angel's blood stained shirt and went white. "Are you . . . ?"

"I'm not hurt, much." She massaged her sore hand. "Delong shot Ethan, and I backhanded him. Broke his nose, I think." She handed the gun over to Officer Denham, who took over for Angel, cuffed Delong, and read him his rights.

She told them what had happened and waited in the car for the authorities to manage the scene. At the first opportunity, Callen took Angel back into town in the Camry.

"Hospital first," she said. "I want to tell Luke, and I think it's time to call my mother."

"Are you sure?" Callen eyed her bloodstained hands.

She smiled. "Okay, resort first, hospital next, then I'll go in and give my statement.

Callen nodded, seeming especially subdued. "I can't believe I let you go back to town with that guy."

"You couldn't have known. I didn't know he had a motive until the professor mentioned that Richard Penghetti had killed Alton's little girl years ago in a drunk-driving accident. Ethan told me that he and Alton had gone to law school together. Then when Alton mentioned that he planned to implicate Bernie in Nick and Justin's murders, I knew. He said you'd talked to him on the way up, but Ethan indicated you hadn't. I knew anyway, since Nick isn't dead and the person who hired Justin is the only one who would think that."

"There's something I don't understand. Why didn't Ethan mention the bad blood between Penghetti and Delong at the cabin?"

Angel shook her head. "He probably didn't remember until he and Delong were face to face. That's the only explanation I can think of. What I don't understand is how Alton Delong could have hired a loser like Justin."

Callen shrugged. "He probably figured he had his tracks covered. Maybe he just got careless."

"Or desperate." She tipped her head back and closed her eyes. "I'm just glad it's over."

Callen dropped her off at the resort. "I'll check in with the chief. Then meet you at the hospital."

Angel called her mother before taking a shower. "Ma," she said when Anna came on the line. "I found Luke."

"What! Is he okay? Where is he?"

Angel answered all those questions and more. Thirty minutes later, she was out the door, heading for the hospital to see her long-lost brother.

Anna Delaney was at her son's bedside the next day. It thrilled Angel to see her so excited and happy. If Anna was upset with Luke or Angel's secrecy, she never said. She just thanked God over and over for bringing back her son. Of course, she welcomed

Kinsey and Marie with open arms and an open heart, thrilled to have two new family members.

One week later, in a cemetery in Colma, California, Angel stood with her mother, Callen, and Luke while Ethan's body was lowered into the ground. His family—a wife, a daughter and a son, and their children—bowed their heads while the pastor prayed.

Angel's gaze scanned the cemetery, looking for Cade. He'd be there among the family, students, and colleagues. She knew that for certain. She also knew that neither she nor Callen nor any of the attending officers would be able to identify him.

Even though she'd be eternally grateful to Cade for letting Luke go free, he should have been the one being laid to rest, not Ethan. But life was full of injustices. At least they had the man responsible for hiring Justin and for hiring Cade to kill the witness and the guard. Already they had more than Angel's testimony in the case against Alton Delong. They had concrete evidence and motive. The signature and prints on the contract where the cell phones had been purchased bore Richard Penghetti's forged name and Alton Delong's fingerprints.

When the service was over, they headed for the airport. Luke would go back to his job in Coeur d'Alene as Luke Delaney rather than Thomas Sinclair. Callen needed to get back to wrap up the details of this bizarre and complicated investigation. Angel and Anna would stay on at Gabby's for several days before heading back to Sunset Cove.

When she got back home, Angel would officially start at her old job with the Sunset Cove police department, where she would put in for detective. Callen hadn't mentioned marriage since he'd left for Portland. He hadn't even talked about it when they'd taken the romantic dinner cruise on the lake in Coeur d'Alene the night before coming to California. Maybe he'd changed his mind. Maybe he thought she was too headstrong. Maybe he couldn't handle being married to a cop.

She'd have to ask him when she got home—and maybe, just maybe, this time if he asked her, she'd say yes.